MIKE McCRARY

THE UNSTABLE ONE

Cover by www.onegraphica.com/

THE UNSTABLE ONE

MIKE MCCRARY

To all the good people in my life, and most of the bad ones.

It is madness for sheep to talk peace with a wolf. –
Thomas Fuller

CHAPTER 1

NOAH POURS himself the last drink of his life.

Drains it, then pours one last one for Kate.

They don't always work together, management prefers the husband and wife work separate shifts, but it does happen from time to time. The entire bar and restaurant could easily be automated, but humans still find enjoyment in the pursuit of attractive humans, and Kate and Noah more than qualify. The illusion starts to crumble if the patrons know they are married, so they're scheduled different hours. Noah and Kate are fully aware of this.

Don't love it, don't hate it.

It simply is.

They've got bills to pay.

Noah and Kate are thankful to work at all. Kate lost one of her other jobs, a checkout gig at a store closer to the house, because of *automation redun-*

dancies. That's what they told her. Noah lost his ride-share gig for the same reason.

Noah wipes down the counter and waits for his wife to finish her paperwork. Ever since they first met, they had shared a drink at the end of their shifts. Fate brought them together at this moderately fancy downtown steak house a few years ago. A flash of eyes. Infatuated smiles. A chemical connection slammed into them like a hurricane.

They were studying at the state university, both care of the GI Bill, and they earned rent slinging sauce and serving finely prepared meat at the before mentioned moderately fancy place of employment.

Kate studied economics and finance. She even interned at an investment management firm one summer. Truly enjoyed the behavioral economics side of it.

Restaurant and hotel management for him. The hospitality trade fits his personality.

On that night a while back, Noah had poured himself a drink and proceeded to drink it down without offering one to his new coworker with the soul-melting gaze.

"Truly some rude shit, man," she said, holding back a smile.

"Dammit." Noah mumbled, stuttered, fumbled, then immediately offered her a drink, along with a thick slice of apologetic charm. She accepted, bit her lip, then gave him a thumbs-up.

That was it.

It was all over for him.

Her too, but she'd never admit it.

Tonight, in step with their tradition, Kate throws back her shot, bites her lip, then pops a thumbs-up into the air. A lot has happened over the years, but a lot has remained the same.

Still a hurricane-style chemical collision.

Fellow employees passing by want to make a joke but know better. Some want to stop and bitch about work, but they see this is a moment not to be messed with.

The intoxicating smell of a good steak prepared well fills the air. Sizzles and pops sound off from the kitchen, along with the occasional chorus of profanity from the staff. Noah is convinced his skin will forever hold the stink of whiskey, red wine and locally brewed beer. Her chestnut brown hair will always smell of grilled meat. Hands will forever hold the scent of loaded baked potatoes. Their personal pheromone.

Kate's fingers gently graze his booze-soaked hands as she locks her eyes with his.

"I have to pump and dump now, asshole."

"Apologies." Noah grins, then pours himself another.

Playfully, she shoves him away before gliding

off to finish shutting down her station. Noah spreads his fingers out on the bar. He likes the feel. The cool stone and its tiny imperfections comfort him. Finding some calm in the storm as the memory of that night plays in his mind. A smile spreads while recalling a lot of the nights since.

During the ride home, Noah feels all the tension he's stored in his broad shoulders. During a dinner rush his muscles always tighten. They crank up as the hours pass. Shoulders become earrings. His shoulders are the keepers of all his bullshit. Refusing to play along with his cover-up.

Kate reaches over, digging a thumb into the area that needs her work the most. She worries that he hides it all. His grinding thoughts. His concerns. Not wanting to talk about it. At least not in any serious way.

A tough nut to crack, they've said about him.

But on their first real date they'd stayed up all night talking, laughing. A date so rare she hadn't wanted it to end. He took her to a cheap, greasy, awesome hamburger paradise near campus. A place that used candles and cheap red tablecloths as mechanisms for charm delivery. They snuck in some wine, pouring it in the joint's somewhat clean soft drink cups.

She asked about his family.

"They practiced aggressive neglect," he said with that wonderful smile of his.

She asked about his experience in the military, wondering if it was that different from hers.

"Was told they'd make a man out of me."

"How's that working out?"

"Not well."

She laughed, taking a sip of her horrific wine. "You know what? You're like a playground wrapped in barbed wire."

Noah couldn't argue. Guilty on all counts. But, after that night, Noah did let Kate in.

Forever and always.

Kate turns up the radio as they continue the long commute home after work. It's one of the few stations left in the world. Mostly talking head paranoid political bullshit, but at night it still plays classic hits from the early 2000s, with some foot-stompers from the '80s and '90s sprinkled in. They share the belief that music after 2025 is nothing short of shit. Music snobbery is the best.

Noah grips the wheel as Kate hits that spot in his back.

She'll work on it more later, but this will get them home.

They talk all the time about getting one of those fancy driverless SUVs. Noah ignores the fact those are the reason he lost one of his jobs. Still, they are nice. The self-driving ones all the soccer moms so casually yammer on and on about at the restaurant during lunch shifts. It's the fantasies that keep you going sometimes. He hates that they have to drive back and forth in this beaten-down car. The upkeep has been tough on their income. The two new tires a month ago almost crushed them. Transmission last year did crush them—still paying that off at almost forty percent interest.

"Stop," she tells him.

"What?"

"Tap pause on your churning brain."

"Love to." Gives her a half-smile. "Can't help it."

"We'll get there."

He nods. They're doing the best they can. The bills are no joke. The debt from when the girls were born is crushing. The problems with the house are mountains he can't climb. The hole in the roof. The ancient water heater. The air conditioner that went shithouse last summer. The neighborhood. Gunshots from the disenchanted rednecks. Homeless wandering during the day. All those, and the potential problems they don't even know about yet spin in an endless loop.

"Not sure about that." Noah's voice fades. "We should be further along in life. The girls—"

"Come on, baby."

He stops, then starts again. Rarely does he come out and say it. "I want them to have more, that's all." His words are low and steady. "Want them to have it better."

Noah and Kate both dropped out of college when the girls were born. They'll go back and finish—they know they will—but they want the kids to get a little older. They dream of putting some money together. Paying some things off. She has less to go with her BA in Finance, so she will go back first.

"Hey." She turns his chin toward her. Eyes warm. Heart open. "We will get there. Our way. Nobody can stop us. Got it?"

She pushes his chin back to the road. He nods with zero conviction.

"Okay?" Kate presses.

"Yes." Noah smirks. "One fine day, we will be super okay."

Kate shakes her head. "Here's an idea." She turns down the radio then whispers into his ear. "After the sitter leaves—"

"Can't afford the sitter either."

"After the sitter leaves," she says, booming the word *after,* "how about we play a little?"

He grins wide. "Yeah?"

"Yeah." She plays with the back of his neck. "You dig the MILFs, right?"

They giggle like horny teenagers.

"My new favorite." Noah kisses her hand.

Kate smiles big. Looking out the window, she watches the country farmland blur by as they put some distance between them and the city, hurtling toward the outer edges. This time of night, the highway is eerily empty. Maybe the occasional trucker, but more times than not it's an open road under the glow of the moon. The sky is big and open, dark and deep. Stars litter the evening canvas holding strong against the relentless night.

From the corner of her eye, something catches Kate's attention.

Something odd.

There's a strange pulse of a glow floating above and to the right of their car.

A perfect small hole of white light cutting into the night. More perfect than a star. Not massive, only the size of a baseball, but it's holding steading while speeding along with their car. She missed it before, lost among the stars.

The white glow lowers, now hovering parallel with her window. Eye level with Kate, though a few car lengths away. Still keeping pace with them. She looks over at the speedometer; they're going a little over eighty.

Kate squints, processing.

Too close to the ground for a plane. Too nimble for anything like that. Maybe a drone.

Why would a drone be out here?

Also, the light looks like part of a vague shadow of an outline. Something bigger than any drone she's ever seen. The moonlight allows a faint view of the edges. They seem smooth in spots then jagged in others.

Kate's mouth opens slightly, lips parted, but no words escape. Kate always considers everything before speaking. She stops playing with the back of Noah's neck.

Outside the window, the glow grows brighter and brighter. The color changes. Shifts to a bloodred portal of light. Searing. Hurts to look at in the night. Then, the bloodred light goes dark as quickly as it burned bright.

She turns off the radio.

"What?" Noah asks. "What's up?"

Kate turns, locking eyes with her husband.

"I don't know."

A machinelike whirl vibrates the entire car.

A whispered zip shreds the peace. Something slams into the passenger side. A bone-rattling jolt as if the car collided with a two hundred mile an hour gust. Seatbelts catch hard, snapping them back into their seats.

The steering wheel rips, spinning free from Noah's grasp.

Another whispered zip.

The car goes airborne.

Turning. Rolling. Each flip gaining momentum. Steel caves in. Bending. Crunching. Tiny shards of glass fly past their faces as the windows blow out. Their heads whip back and forth. Eerie moments of silence fill in the gaps as the car finds the peace of air, only to be brought back to the horror of metal connecting with concrete. A nightmare out of control. The twisted car rips up the earth as it tears into an open field off the side of the highway.

Kate's seatbelt unlatches.

Her body is thrown free from the car.

Noah's fingers helplessly reach out for her. His seatbelt comes undone. He's tossed around the inside of the car like dice. Shattering bones crack inside of him as his body beats against the interior of the car.

The car skids along the grass on its roof, cutting up the ground before slowing to a stop. Tires spin wildly then slow into a loose wobble. Fluids pour from the hood forming puddles on the ground. Steam plumes. Stink of burnt rubber and gas. A violent silence now fills the cool night air.

Kate's still body lies broken in the wet grass.

Noah fights to breathe as his blood spills.

Looking down, he sees a severed scrap of steel jammed into his stomach. A piercing pain he didn't know was possible. His thoughts fight the fog. His thoughts are of the girls. Their twin girls. The day they were born. Playing on the living room floor. How sweet they smelled from their bath. How soft they were as he kissed them goodbye before leaving to go to work. Fragments of memories scream through his dying mind. Halting on a single memory of Kate. A replay of their last drink together.

A silver car stops on the highway. Electric. Driverless.

Noah's grip on consciousness is slipping. Through tunneled vision he sees a tall man step out from the car. Noah can't manage a single word. Begs his body to move, but it cannot. A useless soul in a broken shell.

Noah's eyes shut.

CHAPTER 2

His eyes struggle to open.

Lids flutter like butterfly wings.

They slow to a blink, still working to find moisture. As his sight comes back online, confusion takes over. He's in a room, a room he does not recognize. The walls. The smell. The feel. Nothing's familiar.

No idea where he is.

No memory of how he got here.

Heart pounding. Gut-twisting rips of fear. He's covered with a thin coat of sweat. There's a burning radiating up from his forearm. Rubbing it only makes it worse.

His eyes dart while trying to control his bouncing thoughts.

This room is a top five shithole. Windows are blacked out with dirt and grime, partially covered with thin rags posing as curtains. He's in a bed.

The sheets have some kind of film to them that sticks and peels away from his bare skin. Swallowing back the sickness, he tries not to think about what that *kind of film* might be. Throwing back the sheets, he jumps up from the bed.

Too fast.

His head spins into a tornado hell. Ears ring. His grinding stomach is now full-on nausea. There's some kind of tasteless coating running along his tongue and on his teeth. He's dressed in only a pair of plain white boxers.

Room feels hot and cold at the same time.

Looking around, he sees dark, rich stains dug deep into the carpet. Fairly sure those have nothing to do with him. The room feels more like the set of a bad play than an actual structure. Ancient wallpaper filled with large piss-yellow flowers that have faded almost to the point of nonexistence peels away from the walls. Steady streams of muffled profanity sound from the next room.

A dog barks its nuts off nearby.

His knees wobble underneath him as he struggles to find his bearings. He plants his hand down hard on the bedside table looking for stability. The spinning, the pain, it's starting to slow but still present. The burning from his forearm starts up again, evolving into a throbbing itch of healing.

Looking down, he sees there's a fresh tattoo on his forearm.

It's a classic devil face design about three inches in diameter. The devil has a black mohawk with a cigar jammed in its toothy grin. Its reddish edges are raised, and the whole thing is covered in a clear coating. Running from the devil's face are purplish vein-like streaks. Carefully, he touches it with his fingertip.

"The hell?" He grinds his teeth. The pain nearly made him jump out of his skin.

There's something stranger than the tattoo. Something more troubling.

He can't remember anything.

Squeezing his eyes tight, he tries to force a memory. A simple one.

Any memory.

He doesn't even remember his name.

He can't bring up any detail from yesterday. From last night. Nothing from last year or even childhood. It's all black. An empty tomb where a life should be. Nothing about friends. Where he's from. Family...

Nothing.

Opening his eyes once again, he takes a deep breath. His hands shake. He shakes them back.

Panic helps no one. He's sure someone told him that.

Turning toward his left, he sees a large, round table that seems to defy physics by simply standing. One leg cracked, while the other three are barely hanging on. Resting on top of the table are various items he's also never seen.

A half-filled black trash bag is lumped on the table. Two prescription bottles sit next to the bag. One has a red top, the other green. Next to the pills sits a tall glass of water with beads of sweat dripping, pooling under the glass.

There's a stack of cash. Looks to be twenties from where he stands, the top bill at least. There's also an older phone. He squints, then recognizes the phone is the one he heard people losing their shit about a couple of years ago. Excitement rises inside of him. He remembers something. It's the twentieth anniversary edition of the little phone that changed the entire world. Nostalgia is an insanely powerful marketing drug. It's not his, he's fairly sure, but he can't help but think it's kinda cool.

A rip of pain tears inside his head putting him down on his knees.

Like someone hit him in the back of the head. The worst of it charges hard from the base of his skull, stemming from a place between the occipital bone and lambdoid suture, near the sagittal suture, then spreading out like a jackknifed manure spreader into his entire face and brain.

Between gnashed teeth he breathes in deep. In and out. He takes a moment to collect himself.

Through agony-induced tears, he spots one more item on the table.

A note.

He rubs his face. Stops cold. Nothing about his face feels familiar. He shrugs it off as something that can't be. The pain is making him crazy. With an inhuman noise, he pulls himself up from the floor moving toward the table with the grace of drunk two-year-old. He picks up the note. It's printed in large font with simple words and quick sentences.

Your name is Markus Murphy. You're safe. Get dressed. Take the items on the table. Leave this room quickly. Take 2 pills from the green bottle every 2 hours for the pain. Take 2 pills from the red bottle in the morning. Then another 2 at night. You will receive a call about a job. You should accept it.

Murphy feels fear ramping up again. His forearm aches. His head pounds. Chugging some water, he shrugs, then picks up the bottle with the green top. He pops two pills, hoping the note's pain relief promise is legit. Or, at the very least, that they will help un-fuck his head a little. The name Markus Murphy feels familiar and unfamiliar at the same time. Not his, maybe, but it could be. He feels he's known by another name.

There's another feeling.

A prickling sense he's being watched. Turning, scanning the room, his mind comes back to a somewhat normal place. He sees nothing, but he's fairly sure they can put a camera up an ant's ass these days.

"Shit," he mutters to himself.

What day is it?

How long have I been here?

He grabs the phone. Hands shaking, he taps the glass, lighting up the screen. Can't remember yesterday's date—or who he was yesterday—but the date the phone displays feels like it's in the ballpark. It's more the time that has him puzzled.

It's 3:36 in the morning.

Looking around, he attempts the impossible task of gathering his thoughts. There are memories now, maybe, but they are hard to process. Loose fragments, soft and impossible to grab onto. None of them seem to piece together. Feels as if Murphy is viewing different movies, in different languages, running together at the same time.

Emotions swing and sway without weight or context. He wants to crumble and cry and punch someone's face in while he's doing it. Everything mashes together.

Sirens wail outside.

The screams next door grow louder. Angry people are fighting. The dog's bark is now like a roar. Thumps and thuds rattle the thin walls. A picture of a three-legged horse falls from the filthy wall. Its glass cracks as the corner hits the carpet.

He looks back over the note, rereading the words *you're safe* then the somewhat contradictory *leave this room quickly*.

Tires screech outside.

Headlights flood in through the window.

His heart thuds inside his chest even though he knows he's done nothing wrong—at least he thinks not. Feels like a murderous mob is out to get him and he needs to move fast. He grabs the back of his head. The pain stabs at him, then flutters, fading out into nothing without warning.

Maybe the meds from the helpful invisible people are doing something.

Opening the trash bag, he finds clothes neatly folded and stacked. He changes into a black T-shirt and a pair of jeans. Feels like the T-shirt could fall apart at any moment and the jeans wear like sandpaper, but it all fits. He slips on black socks then a pair of thin-soled running shoes.

A loud crack outside.

As if the door from the next room was knocked down. Hard voices bellow orders that vibrate inside the walls. Murphy shoves everything from the table into the trash bag. As he does, his hand brushes against something at the bottom. His breathing stops. His heart freezes.

His trembling hand removes a gun from the bag.

As he grips the gun, two tiny pinhole lights on the left and right of the gun's sight change from blank to a solid green. The biometric readers in the grip and trigger have identified him.

Green means go.

This gun knows him.

Murphy knows this gun is a G19 Generation Seven Glock, 9x19mm caliber. Has a mag capacity of seventeen, weighs twenty-one ounces fully loaded, roughly nineteen unloaded, and has a laser sight installed in the grip. From twenty-five yards out he can keep his shots grouped to the size of a baby's fist.

He knows all this.

All without a shred of doubt, and with no idea how.

You're safe, they said.

CHAPTER 3

Murphy cinches up the trash bag.

There's a nibble of a chill to the air.

Can't help but think it feels nice.

The darkness outside the room seems to swallow him. Above him, holes are punched into the night by streetlights peeking out between towering buildings. He's in an alley, somewhere. The street is dry, with random puddles, along with trash piled up here and there. Murphy moves as fast as he can away from the room.

Sounds of a small war echo behind him.

A battle being waged in the room that was next door to his. The voices are loud. Sounds of aggression are way too close. Fairly sure he heard someone take a punch before he left the room.

He doesn't want to run, but he walks fast, turning and checking behind him every few seconds while holding the trash bag tight. There's fear-induced curiosity that he can't control, but he's also trying to make sure no one is following him.

A man's voice calls out.

"Hey," the voice barks. "Hey, trashman."

Footsteps quicken behind him.

Turning back, he sees two large shadows soak up what little light there is. Murphy decides running has become his best option. He bolts down the alley. Dodging potholes. Turning corners, burning down straightaways. He hits a barely lit street. A truck races past him, centimeters from ending his life.

He takes a hard right, banking off a wall.

Spinning, his ankles pop as he trips over a trash can landing almost face-first on the cement. He pushes off the street, springing up to his feet. Murphy pumps his legs harder and harder, like pistons firing. He runs faster and faster. Pushing himself to the brink. Surprised with his speed.

More surprised with his lack of fatigue.

He takes a turn with no sense of direction. Occasionally, he looks behind him, never stopping to think about what is happening. There's too much to process. Questions too scary to ask.

For now.

He runs until his thighs burn and his lungs pump acid. His heart beats against his ribs like a hammer. He's impressed with how far he's been able to run at this pace. Yet, he somehow knows he can go even harder.

Spilling out from a maze of blurred walls and lights, he realizes he's in a large city.

He's been running all-out for blocks and blocks. Now he sees nothing but towering buildings and streets lined with various businesses. Hints of the night's sky peek out here and there. He passes by the homeless. Blazes past high-end coffee shops and white tablecloth restaurants that span the spectrum of global cuisine. Signs of the split between the wealthy and poor surround him in all directions.

He thinks he's in New York.

There's an ache of a feeling that he's been here many times before.

Murphy eases up his pace, slowing into a jog, then to a walk. He hasn't heard anyone behind him in a while. As he slows, he sees a bench at a bus stop surrounded by glass walls to shield the public from the elements. Maybe he'll take the bus. Maybe he won't. Each moment is writing a path to the next.

His legs and hands tremble. He needs to collect himself.

Needs to hole up somewhere and think, but he realizes he has nowhere to go. No place that he remembers at least. Maybe he has a house somewhere. Maybe someone is waiting for him. A family. Friends. A girlfriend. A boyfriend. Hell, a dog for Christ's sake.

Something buzzes and blips from inside the trash bag.

Murphy fishes around inside the bag, moving past the Glock to the lit-up phone buzzing like an angry hornet. The phone given to him by them—whoever that may be. There's a number stretching across the screen that says New York City, NY underneath. A small sliver of Murphy relaxes. Well, at least maybe he got the city right.

Murphy answers the call.

"Markus?" The man's voice is like thick gravy. "You Markus Murphy?"

"Yeah—yes." Surprised he's able to get any words out.

"Okay then. Your lucky day," Gravy Voice says with little to no enthusiasm. "Had a guy quit tonight right after his shift, the prick. We need someone for tomorrow."

Murphy thinks back to the note. Someone calling him about a job.

"You there?"

"Yeah, sure." Murphy gathers himself. This is the closest thing to a living, breathing information source. "Where do I need to go?"

"Jesus. You were just here—like a few goddamn hours ago."

"What?" Murphy's heart sinks.

"Johnny Psycho's. Ask for Johnny." Gravy Voice mutters something inaudible, then, "West 52nd. Hell's Kitchen. Be here at eight tomorrow night. Don't fuck it up."

"Wait—"

The call has already ended.

Murphy thinks again of the note. He assumes this means he accepted the job, even though the actual words never left his mouth. The idea he's being led around by the nose gnaws at him. Hates it but doesn't see he has any great options. At the moment, everyone on the planet knows more than he does.

Murphy looks up at the night sky that's beating back the morning.

Is this it? he thinks. *Is this the rest of my life now?*

Welcome to the unknown.

A flash of a memory screams past his mind's eye.

Fast. Without warning. Smiles. Laughter. A man and woman at a bar sharing a drink. She has amazing eyes. He's tall with broad shoulders. Murphy's mind takes in the moment. Flickers of joy tickle his wire-tight brain. These people in the memory, the man and woman, he feels these are people he knows. Their happiness is palatable. There's an energy to this. This is a memory so real he can feel the strength of their connection even through the fuzzy replay in his mind. The woman's amazing eyes are big and filled with something that can only be described as unfiltered affection. The woman laughs, bites her lower lip, then gives him a thumbs-up.

Are they friends of his?

Family?

"Hey there," a man's voice says. "You're a fast one, trashman."

CHAPTER 4

Two walking walls of muscle move in fast.

Both large men, but one is larger than the other.

Murphy's fingers tingle off the sight of them.

They are standing close. Too close. Murphy can feel the warmth of their breath as they loom over him. There's a stiff stink of beef and beer. Murphy sits motionless on the bench. His heart was pounding at an alarming rate only seconds ago, but now, to his surprise, his pulse is slowing down. A strange calm is coming over him. As if a switch has been flipped. He catches a reflection of himself in the mirrored glass of the bus stop.

A part of him doesn't recognize who he sees.

Another part finds comfort in the sight.

There's a hint of familiarity, yet something is off. Different. It's the eyes. The blue eyes staring back at him are cold and unfamiliar. A distant stare removed from the here and now. It is more what's behind those eyes. This guy? This Murphy reflected in the glass? There's an untethered aggression frolicking deep inside the meat of this one's brain.

He turns back to the large men, alternating his focus between their thick hands and their wide shoulders. The strongest indicators of where potential harm might stem from.

"What did you hear?" the bigger of the two asks.

"What?" Murphy isn't sure what's going on, but they stormed the room next to him. "Where?"

"Oh you know, trashman." The bigger one gives Murphy a slap to the face. On the lighter side, but that slap was designed as a warm-up. A show of who's in charge. "You hear what was going on over there?"

Murphy feels a part of him slide.

Then a click inside his head. Something finding its proper place.

He tries to stand up. He's shoved down to the bench immediately. Hard, like a disobedient animal. Murphy's phone slips from his hand, falling to the curb. He hears the glass screen crack.

The least of his problems, but still, it pisses him off. Looking up from the bench, Murphy sees guns strapped to the sides of their thick bodies. Smith &

Wessons. Ready to go, lying in wait underneath their thin, cheap jackets.

"You were next door, right?" chirps the smaller of the two mountains.

Murphy's eyes slip to his trash bag then back to them.

"You catch what was going on in there, trashman?"

Murphy shakes his head *no.* His face an icy void.

"You call anybody? Tell anybody about anything?" The bigger one stabs his sausage digit at Murphy's forehead. "Because that would be kinda bad, Noah."

Everything in Murphy shuts down.

Noah?

That name—Noah—there's something to it.

The sound of it digs deep. The name echoes in a distant place inside his mind. One he can't fully access, but the emotion around the name carries a pulse. One that's gaining strength.

"What?" Murphy asks. "What did you call me?"

The muscle boys stare back at him as if they've turned to stone. Statues on the street. They seem to fade for a fraction of a second. A flicker to their shape. They stand motionless, frozen, only for a moment as they look back at him like stuffed grizzly bears.

They disappear.

As if swallowed by the wind.

Then reappear in a blink of Murphy's eye.

"You call anybody? Tell anybody about anything?" The bigger one stabs his sausage digit at Murphy's forehead. "Because that would be kinda bad, Murphy."

An exact repeat—save for the switch of the name.

Noah to *Murphy.*

Murphy's eye twitches. Something new is building behind his thousand-yard stare. A wave of confidence is crashing in as all his doubt and fear rolls out. The ache in his head is rising again. His devil tat burns with a new itch.

He feels different.

"*Kinda bad*? Damn, you don't say." Murphy taps his lips with his finger.

"Yeah, we do say." The smaller one looks to his partner, his limited brain chewing on something. "I know you were just next door and all. Wrong place, wrong time and all, but..."

The muscle boys share a look. As if they've communicated a question between them and a decision has been rendered. Murphy can see it all over their faces. They've ruled that he needs to go away.

No idea what kind of shit they were into next door, but Murphy also does not need to find out.

The pain behind his eyes is building, compounding, nearing the point of blinding. He shoves it all down. Needs to dig deep into the here and now and fight for some footing.

If he wants to survive.

"Sorry, brutha." The bigger of the two puts one paw on Murphy's shoulder and the other on the gun under his jacket. "Wrong place, wrong time, like he said. Bad shit does indeed happen to good people."

There's a shift in Murphy's thinking. Complete shift in his being.

"May I..." Words form in his mind, but they don't feel like they are his own. "May I make one last request, kind sirs?"

They nod, confusion setting in.

"Thank you." Murphy conjures some oddly timed puppy eyes. "Can I hear you scream?"

The muscle boys aren't sure they heard that right.

Murphy fires up from the bench.

The crown of his head smashes under the big one's chin like a piston. The jawbone crunches. Blood spits. Teeth fall. Probably removed some of his tongue. Murphy moves without a hint of hesitation, without fear or a fraction of thought, yet in absolute control.

Unwavering confidence in his violence.

Murphy spins, plants his feet wide forming a

strong base with superior leverage. He releases a swarm of punches. Machine-gun thumps of fists on flesh. A hard palm to the face. A nose snaps. Ribs crack. Fast, zero effort wasted, and over before it started. Murphy puts the bigger one through the mirrored glass. Shattering shards bounce off the street. Glitter in the moonlight. Murphy steps back, watching the big slab of a human wilt to the pavement, crunching in the fallen glass.

Murphy kicks the smaller one's knee, popping it in a direction it was never intended to go. A pain-scream rips from his lips. Grabbing him by the collar, Murphy pulls him down while shoving his other hand into his trash bag. Murphy jams the Glock into the smaller one's mouth, keeping him down on his knees while standing over him. He pushes the barrel past his teeth, sliding along the tongue heading down his throat.

Murphy tightens his finger on the trigger.

Sights are lit.

Green means go.

He looks into the bulging, terrified eyes of the man down on his knees. Terror-tears form as he gags on Murphy's gun barrel. Murphy blinks, feeling his own eyes starting to fill. His vision clouds. He tries to blink them clear. Murphy holds the gun down the man's throat.

Murphy can't believe what he's doing.

Doesn't even seem real.

Like he's watching another version of him. His finger squeezes tighter. Only a minimal amount of additional pressure will blow out the back of this man's skull. Murphy knows it. He's sure he's done it before.

He called me *Noah.*

A hostile hoard of new ideas storm his thoughts. A new point of view offered inside his switchblade mind. A part of Murphy screams for him to stop.

No!

Murphy's arm begins to shake. The coiled muscles of his forearm wrestle under the skin. The gun feels like it suddenly weighs a hundred pounds.

Murphy's brain cuts into fragments again. Images bounce and blur. Reality seems to fade, pop, then return. A muffled plea slips around the barrel of the gun. The man's pleas for his life bring Murphy back to the here and now.

This is a human being.

A person. A person who's afraid for his life.

The man's face changes.

Right before Murphy's eyes. The man's face flashes to that of a demon-like being. A devil. Not of this earth. Eyes that burn white. Skin the color of the darkest of red wine. Murphy's mouth opens. An inaudible whisper slips out. He doesn't even know what he said.

The man's skin bubbles, as if cooking on the bone. Murphy squeezes his eyes tight, shaking his head back and forth hoping to shake himself free from whatever this is.

He's seeing things.

This is a breakdown.

His mind is worse than he thought. He's the owner of a broken brain that's now digging into a fresh bag of tricks. His own eyes are betraying him. Showing him things that are simply not real. A part of him tries to reason with himself. Tells himself this isn't happening.

The other part of Murphy couldn't care less.

He pulls the trigger.

"No!" Murphy screams, trying to control himself.

The kick of the Glock rattles the smaller one's teeth. Murphy's arm vibrates, feeling the power of the weapon rattle his entire body. The tears in his eyes finally give way, rolling hot down Murphy's face. He pulls the Glock out from the smaller one's lips.

The man leans back holding his face. He's still alive. Shaken. Shock stealing speech from him, but his head remains in one piece.

Murphy can only stare at him.

What the hell?

The gun fired—that much Murphy knows—but it wasn't a real bullet. A tester round, maybe? A *dummy pop* used in training. Used to call them *blanks* years ago, only much safer now. Murphy doesn't have time to question why his gun is loaded with testers. He's more deeply concerned with the part of him that could pull the trigger as if swatting a bug. Horrified he pulled the trigger so casually when he thought the bullets fired true.

"Run." Murphy's eyes are crazed. Mind set ablaze. "Fly away, lucky boy."

The smaller one gathers his larger friend up off the street. They run like no one has ever run before, disappearing out into the night. Murphy slumps down to the street bracing himself with one hand on the bus bench. In and out, his labored breaths are deep and steady.

The world moves in slow motion, as if he's being pulled from a car crash. Searching for calm after sudden chaos. Everything is wrong. Everything feels shattered. Pieces of him are missing, replaced with new ones that don't fit. Jammed together with ones that don't belong.

A car starts up across the street.

Murphy jumps, his heart shooting up into his throat. Headlights kick on as a large SUV pulls away. Nothing remarkable about the car. Couldn't make out the driver, if there was one at all, or how many occupants were inside. Nothing for Murphy to hang on to. After the car passes, the street goes back to the stillness of the hour.

Fear is the new normal.

A new fear of himself.

Tears continue to fall down his trembling face. He searches for comfort, softly repeating to himself that everything is okay. Soothing words spoken to a child waking from a nightmare. If he tells himself the lie long enough, perhaps it will ring true. Wiping underneath his eyes, he rubs the hot tears between his fingers. He looks at his fingertips. Murphy feels his world tilt.

They are smeared with blood.

His sight becomes swallowed in black.

CHAPTER 5

Murphy is weightless, wedged somewhere between consciousness and something else.

Floating in a pool of warm milk under the cover of darkness.

Comforting, like he's been here before.

Every so often, he feels pressure applied to his arms and legs. A press to the neck. To the temple. There's no pain, more like fingertips pressing down on his skin.

As if this is common.

His mind has found some stability. More stable than it has been recently, at the very least. Insane to consider, but it's as if his thoughts are not really there at all. Wisps of images, rumors of ideas with nothing sticking. Thinking is not a function necessary at the moment. No thoughts carrying any form of weight. As if his brain has pressed pause leaving him on a black screen.

He feels his heart thump.

Tries to count the beats but loses track. Every expansion of his lungs taking in air feels earned, and he's fairly sure he can pick up a rhythm to the blood flowing through his veins.

There's a sensation of being lifted up.

Of being moved.

The pin prick of a needle to this thigh.

One thought occurs to him. More a vision. No, correction, this is a memory. One that carries some substance. Some real weight. He's seen this before. Recently. Now, however, he can make out every note of the music playing. Each smell has an identity, a familiarity. The scent of red wine with a whiff of steak cooked to perfection. In front of him are two people, a man and a woman he's sure he knows but can't place.

Attractive. Seem nice. Friendly.

Smiling and laughing while having a drink at the bar of what looks like a fairly nice steak house. They're completely fixated on one another. Eyes flaring, sharing then holding their gaze. No place on the planet they'd rather be. The man pours her a drink. The woman laughs, bites her lower lip, then gives him a thumbs-up.

Murphy feels himself smile.

An internal embrace with happiness.

There's a new, more aggressive memory entering the fray. One where he recognizes himself. A man with similar features to Murphy stands in a house that overlooks a beach. Muted sounds of crashing waves mumble through the walls. Smell of ocean air fills the room. Bright sunshine cuts shafts of light through the half-open plantation shutters. He is dressed in a dark suit. Black with an electric blue tie. He's holding a gun in one hand. A bottle of whiskey in the other. Dead bodies litter the floor. Blood splatters decorate the walls. His shoulder aches. Whiffs of gunpowder mix in with the intoxicating smell of the ocean. An older woman stands in the corner. She's screaming at him. The man drinks his whiskey from the bottle.

Another needle slips into the meat of his shoulder. Flush of warmth spreads.

His mouth goes dry before the smack of a metallic taste coasts his tongue.

The memory fades.

Thoughts without weight resume.

His mind settles into its dark pause.

CHAPTER 6

Murphy's eyes struggle to open.

Lids flutter like butterfly wings.

Slowing to a blink, they work overtime seeking moisture. As his sight comes back online, his mind drifts into a cloud of confusion. This room, he does not recognize.

No idea where he is.

No memory of how he got here.

Murphy fires straight up in bed.

As his eyes scan the room, he can't help but be relieved this room is nothing like the last place. Massive improvement, actually. This room is clean, sleek, and sharp. Feels expensive. The air has been set at a crisp, cool temperature, and damn, it is comfortable. The walls are painted in warm tones instead of peeling paper with piss-yellow faded flowers. He's dressed in silk, black pajamas with large red dots. Hates to admit he likes them.

He feels rested.

Energized. He can't understand how that's possible. There's an overwhelming, unexplainable sense of calm to him.

That calm is cut short as his thoughts shift.

He digs his fingers into the bed. Thoughts of last night bubble to the surface. The street. The men chasing him. Memories flood, unable to hold them back. Last night–*oh my God.* It robs the air from his lungs as his mind clicks into place. The memory of what he did.

I beat a man to a pulp.

Tried to kill another one.

His stomach twists into a pretzel. The faces of the two men blur then blend together. The snap of bones echoes. The teeth-rattling boom of that gun. The feelings of rage he possessed last night. Hard to hold it back. A wild dog snapping free from its leash. It came on so fast and without an ounce of effort. He was so comfortable with it all. Part of Murphy struggles to understand.

Where did it come from?

He's unable to reconcile the rage that was so accessible last night. The unthinkable violence that danced on the end of his fingertips. He remembers the words he used. The words he said. The question he asked.

Can I hear you scream?

That wasn't anything he'd ever think to say.

Part of him would never be so cold. So brutal. Another part would never be so cute before taking someone out.

The last thing from last night enters his thoughts.

The final scene from the night fires across his mind. He was bleeding from his eyes.

Frantic, he checks his hands and fingers. They are clean. No signs of blood.

"What the hell?"

This can't be happening. He needs help.

Someone has to be able to help him. A doctor. A hospital. The police.

Anyone.

Murphy's feet hit the floor, ignoring his whirling mind. He bobs and weaves, feet tilting, toes gripping the carpet to find stability. His stomach drops as his hand reaches the door. There's a shift. An undeniable change inside of him. A searing burn rips up from his forearm. The pain in his head stabs like a blade, pushing deeper and deeper. His ears ring. His knees crumble as his body wilts.

Pulling, clawing his fingers into the carpet, Murphy drags himself back toward the bed. As he does, the pain begins to fade with every inch he fights for. The intensity becomes less and less as he gets farther away from the door.

Murphy flips over on his back, his chest

heaving as he fights to find his breath. He feels his heart find its normal beat. His head steadies. The burn in his forearm all but disappears. From his back, he glances toward the room's door.

They don't want him to leave. Not yet at least.

Someone else is in charge.

He's being led around by the nose, and he is not a fan.

His fists grip tight. His heart rate rises again. A distant voice in the back of his mind calls for calm. A voice that wants answers rather than blood.

"The Cash Clash changed everything," a polished voice says.

Murphy's eyes dart around the room. He sits up.

A massive TV that takes up the wall is showing a news show round table. A British gentleman is talking passionately about a crisis. "The worst financial crisis since COVID-19. Makes 2008 look like a bad comedy," he says. He and his counterparts argue back and forth over the outcomes of the crisis. All the damage it has caused and the future damages yet to come. Call it the Cash Clash. They talk about riots in New York last night. They talk about how it happened so fast and came from out of nowhere.

Words like *lives devastated, destruction* and *social unrest.*

Body count.

The torn fabric of American society. The country needs to heal.

The show escalates into political rambling. Shouting. Fingers waving. The noise from the screen now twirls around Murphy's mind. It enters his ears but fails to land in any meaningful way. He pushes himself up from the floor. His body and mind hurt like hell, but there's improvement. It's a low hurdle, but he does feel more together right now. More human. Calm even.

The difference in him is night and day.

His head is still fuzzy around the edges, but not even close to what it was moments ago. Far better than last night at the cheap motel. He hates to think in tired clichés, but he does feel somewhat like a new man. He can't put his finger on what is different, but there is definitely something about him that has changed.

Guilt creeps in.

Guilt for moving past what he did last night so casually. It took all of twenty seconds for him to brush off his acts of violence. As if he forgot about some roaches he stepped on last week. Yet, he sees no need to linger on the memory. Guilt seems like a wasted emotion.

A room service cart is parked at the foot of the bed.

The idea of an amazing hotel breakfast stampedes through the middle of his heart. He imagines the bacon, the eggs, and toast underneath the shiny silver dome. Maybe even an omelet.

Sweet Jesus, let there be an omelet.

The coffee smells like heaven should smell. A freshly brewed pot sits next to the silver pleasure dome. He lifts the lid. Takes a peek.

His heart dances.

A fluffy pillow of an omelet with bacon, cheese and avocado spilling out from the sides. Too much goodness to be contained. Butter drips from thick slices of toast. Murphy tries not to cry. Can't remember the last meal he had. He does recall a technique he heard about. Not sure where, but he was told about a process that was tested with prisoners of war. Reinforcing pain with kindness. Like, say, putting a man on the floor in agony then giving him a lovely breakfast.

Effective.

A table near the window is covered in shadow, but Murphy can see it is filled with various items. He can make out shapes. He can guess what they are but doesn't really want to know for sure.

Murphy pulls open the curtains, not realizing he could just tell them to open. The curtains remind him how they work in a pleasant yet somewhat condescending tone. A gorgeous morning is coming to life just beyond the glass. The sun rising over New York City. His room has a jaw-dropping view of Central Park blanketed in orange and purple tints. Couldn't be any more different from where he was only hours ago.

Or was it days ago?

He passed out.

No idea who moved him or why.

Murphy finds some comfort that he's at least in the same city. Taking a deep breath, he looks to the table. There's a new phone waiting for him along with some other items. Can't help but notice it's the same twentieth anniversary phone, though it's not the same one he had last night. He can still hear the glass screen crack as it hit the street last night. This one is clean, without a scratch. Perfect condition, as if it were pulled straight from the box.

Next to the phone are prescription bottles, with a one page note next to them.

New bottles. Different colors and more of them than last time. One has a yellow lid. One black. Third one is blue. There's another stack of cash. The gun he had before is the same, however. It shines as if someone gave it a good cleaning.

Gone is the trash bag.

In its place is a high-end, black, aluminum suitcase that sits open. As if on display for Murphy to see. It is packed with better, more expensive clothes than before. Seems to be a variety of casual and dress. There's also a pair of jeans, a navy-blue T-shirt folded on the table, black workout socks and a pair of high-dollar sneakers that cost more than a car payment. The T-shirt has the words Johnny Psycho's written in some form of bloodred neon font on the front. A cartoonlike logo of two hands firing off double-barrel middle fingers on the back.

Resting on the shoes is a small note.

YOUR WORK UNIFORM.

Led by the nose, indeed.

His fists tighten once again. Violent thoughts simmer as he picks up the Johnny Psycho's shirt. Gravy Voice is the closest thing he has to a starting point. Murphy decides to begin his work tonight at Johnny Psycho's in Hell's Kitchen.

What time is it?

He taps the phone's screen. Eyes pop wide. *Shit.*

He's lost the entire day.

CHAPTER 7

A DAY GONE.

Vanished.

Was I asleep the whole time?

He struggles to put the events of last night in order. They scatter and turn inside his mind. The last thing he remembers is being in the street. He remembers running. Fleeing the shit motel room. Beating down a man. Almost shooting the other man in the throat. The blood on his fingers. The blood from his eyes. There's a spike of fear. Fear that quickly fades into a vapor, drifting away like smoke from a dying fire.

This differs from before. He's different.

Everything has a different feel to it.

He's not shaking like he did before. His heart is not pounding. The fear is there, but it is underneath something. It is under control rather than the fear controlling him. He's handling this all very well. Surprisingly well. He's not sure that he should be.

Is this becoming normal?

The violence, the blood, is this what I am now?

Murphy picks up the note next to the pills. Same style. Same quick, simple sentences. Same shit about being safe.

Markus Murphy, you are safe. Your medication has been adjusted. Take one of each with food morning and night. Do this then leave to your new job at 8pm. Don't talk about last night. Not with anyone.

Below the message are two images. Pictures. Both printed in color. Both are photos of Murphy asleep. The first is of him asleep in a filthy room with faded flowers on the walls. The room from before. Below that is a photo of him asleep in the plush room he's in right now.

A part of Murphy peels away.

He, of course, knew people were watching him. Trying to control him. But something about seeing full-color, glossy photos of it in action is beyond unsettling. The mind can protect itself from the ugly reality of things, but it is hard for even Murphy's brain to go into safe mode looking at these. He lets the photos drop to the floor as his eyes stare out, as if looking through the walls that hold him captive.

Who the hell is doing this?

What do they want?

Murphy slumps down into the chair, attempting to walk it back. Sifting through the insanity.

What do I know?

What facts do I actually have?

They're watching. They want him to know they are on him. To know that they are in control. Maybe they want him guessing. Off balance. They want him fully aware they are working the strings and moving him along as they see fit.

He looks at the devil tattoo on his arm. The one he can now safely assume *they* gave him. It itches like hell. The spiderlike veins around it have faded. All but disappeared. The redness has become a pinkish hue. A new, fresh coat of cream or ointment has been applied with a clear tape of sorts covering it.

His mind skips back to last night.

While he was sleeping, there was the feeling like he was being moved. Handled. He recalls the prick of needles. The warmth of things. Of chemicals entering his flesh and bloodstream. Fear creeps in again, then fades away just as quickly. As if his brain has trained itself to push it all away upon impact.

He remembers what he saw on his fingertips. The blood that was streaming from his eyes like tears. The idea melts the second it hits his mind, like butter on a hot skillet. He can't hold on to a single thought for more than a moment. Despite all this, there's a layer of calm coating those thoughts. He can't believe he's waging a war between anxiety and calm. One being fought inside the same person. The same head.

His hands shake.

He shakes them back.

They stop. He pours himself a cup of coffee. It's amazing.

He doesn't have much time before his new job —assuming he can make it out of the room without his head blowing up. He knows this new life of his will start with or without him. Taking in a deep breath, he pulls the room service cart closer.

Can't help but feeling like he's letting them win, but he's starving.

A shower would be nice.

Staring at the breakfast, he lets his thoughts hum through a plan. He can't believe his acceptance of all this. How easy it is all becoming. The strange sensation of being disgusted with himself, yet okay with it. A part of him wants to run.

There's another part of him that wants to see what happens next.

Murphy picks up a fork.

The omelet melts as it hits his tongue, just like he hoped it would.

CHAPTER 8

The hotel lobby mirrors the look and feel of his room.

A place designed to impress.

High-end people from around the world roll in with high-end luggage speaking a variety of languages, all looking indifferent to be where they are. Designer clothes. Jewelry that sparkles under the lobby's crystal lighting. Men in burgundy suits with matching ties hold open the doors. Some of the better hotels still staff actual people rather than automate. Studies show that the wealthy enjoy tipping more than originally thought. The ego receives a jolt from seeing gratitude from those with less. Humans serving humans still passes the sniff test for the upper class.

Murphy takes it all in as he cuts a path through the large open floor.

He scans over everyone. Checks their eyes first

to see if they are looking back at him. Wonders if these unknown fans of his that lurk in the night, moving him from place to place, are still here at the hotel. If *they* are on him all the time. He also pays close attention, checking everyone's hands.

Are they empty?

What are they holding?

Are hands holding potential weapons stuffed in pockets out of view?

He makes a lightning-fast assessment of each person. Never pausing his progress toward the men in burgundy at the door. Pushing hard toward the exit without rushing is difficult. A burst of cool night air blows in as they open the doors up ahead then quickly close. He can feel the freedom out there.

So close.

But there will be no freedom until he finds who's pulling his strings. Hates the idea, but he knows he has to play their game until he finds a way to beat it.

When that happens, God help them.

In the middle of the lobby, a four-foot glass vase stuffed with long red roses sits on a massive oak table. Murphy takes note of its size. Takes note because while he might not pick it up easily or push it onto someone, he could put a bullet in the glass to create a helluva diversion if needed. He doesn't bother questioning why he's thinking like this.

"Car?" Murphy hands a short man in burgundy some folded cash.

"Driver or the other thing?"

"Other thing." Murphy has no desire to roll the dice on some chatty-ass driver.

The short man in burgundy nods, squeezes the cash, then holds open the door. They step outside into the cool, crisp air. The streets are packed tight tonight, as with most evenings. Central Park is alive across from the hotel. Murphy can see a decent-sized crowd has gathered at the park. The yelling can be heard even over the honking cars and roaring trucks. Bodies sway, heads bob and jerk, with signs being waved back and forth. Someone with a bullhorn rants a series of chants.

"Hey, man." A bearded man wearing a torn, dirty denim jacket rushes toward Murphy.

Murphy inches his hand closer to the Glock tucked behind his back. Reading the desperation in the bearded man's eyes, he pulls his hand away from the gun.

The much shorter doorman rushes in, holding the bearded man back. "Get out of here," the doorman snaps. "Not today."

"Come on, man," the bearded man says, pointing back toward his yellow cab parked near the entrance. Looks like it's barely functioning. "Gotta eat."

"Take that one, sir." The doorman points Murphy to a white Cadillac with blacked-out windows.

"That's great." The bearded man spits his words as the doorman pushes him back. "How we supposed to scratch out a living with this bullshit?"

"Hey." Murphy looks into the eyes of the angry cab driver. His feelings are mixed. "What does a ride to West 52nd run me?"

"For you? Less than ten, friend."

"Ten? That a joke?"

The driver waves his hands wildly, yells something.

"Fair enough." Murphy stuffs a twenty down into the driver's pants then gives him a hard spank on the ass.

Murphy slides into the backseat of the Cadillac sealing himself off from the rest of the city. He surprised himself back there. Feels an odd, certain sense of accomplishment. Part of him wanted to help while the other would rather shoot the driver than listen to him speak. Finding the midpoint between decent human and complete asshole is something new. A delicate dance no one has bothered to show him the steps.

A tickle starts at the back of his head.

Pinching the bridge of his nose, he closes his

heavy eyes for a moment of peace. He can still hear the muted aggression outside but feels safe inside this contained cocoon of a car.

The doors lock.

The car is empty with a long display that stretches along the bottom of the windshield. No steering wheel on the driver's side. He recalls hearing the companies tried out steering wheels with people-like things made of latex and plastic bolted into the driver's seat. Thought it would make consumers more comfortable during this technological transition. It didn't test well. Creepy as hell.

"Hey, how you doin'?" the car asks in the thickest Brooklyn accent ever. "You a returning customer or what?" The sound of his voice is full-on nails on a chalkboard.

Murphy winces. "Not sure. Feels like I might be."

"Want your saved settings?"

"Anything but you."

A second of silence. Some soft clicks. He sees the small lens on the rearview mirror zero in on him scanning his face. A new voice speaks.

"Hello. Welcome back, Mr. Murphy." The woman's voice is sweet and charming. Like a friendly soul who's happy to be driving you around. "I'm Amy. Where would you like to go today?"

Markus Murphy appears at the bottom of the windshield. No surprise he has no memory of riding in one of these but doesn't doubt that he has. Next to his image is a fake picture of Amy. She's an algorithmic generation of what the car thinks Murphy wants to see. A pleasant, attractive woman in a dorky librarian kind of way, but looks like she's confident where she's going.

"Johnny Psycho's on—"

"West 52nd. Of course. There's bottled water in the door, and I'll load your normal presets as well. Should we stop and purchase your favorite bottle of whiskey?"

Murphy's eyes flare. This car knows more about him than he does.

"What else do you know about me?"

"Pardon?"

"What else can you tell me about me?"

"Privacy restrictions prohibit the usage of data in this manner. Please review our user privacy policy at our website."

"Okay, that's fine."

"Did you want the whiskey?"

"No, no thank you." Murphy looks through the tinted glass, considering the park and the protests. "Can you go around the park first?"

"Certainly. That will add about thirty-six minutes to the drive. Is that okay?"

"Yeah." Checks his phone for the time. "That's fine."

The car pulls out into traffic that moves slightly faster than a spirited stroll. The doorman and the cab driver still go at it outside the hotel. Pushing, fingers pointing, faces red with mouths flapping wide. There's anger in the air. You can taste it. The car speakers play a news program. Murphy recognizes the British voice from the news show playing in his room.

"It was only a few days ago," the British man says. "We don't know everything, do we? Not yet. Not sure who started it. The *how*, uncertain. The *why*, however, is clearer than crystal."

As the car crawls past Central Park, Murphy can see the crowds are not only near the hotel. They are spread out all over the park. Hundreds of people gathered. So much anger out there. Much like the cab driver. These are not tourists or wealthy Manhattanites walking spoiled pets. These are the working class. The heart and soul. People that make this city and country run.

"Markets have fallen forty-eight percent over the last two weeks. The slowing global economy has been tapping the breaks for a while, but this feels like a tipping point. Companies are shutting their doors. Layoffs are stacking up with rumors this is only the beginning. The gap between wealth and poverty..."

As they turn the corner, the park view opens up. In the distance, deeper into the park, Murphy sees plastic strips of yellow police tape stretched across some areas of the park along with barricades blocking off other sections. Officers hold people back. Faces locked in furious screaming. Fists waving. The tension of the streets is felt, even behind the protective glass and metal of the Cadillac.

"People lost their lives in that New York park. Police and civilians. This *Cash Clash*, this *Snobs versus Slobs*. And there have been similar incidents as well. Los Angeles yesterday, four dead and another ten seriously hurt. Dallas, Chicago more of the same. London, France are seeing..."

Murphy doesn't have a solid memory of any of this but feels he heard about it all. He can't picture anything about the events being described, yet nothing about it seems new to him. As if someone is recapping what he already knew but has forgotten.

"There's a war brewing."

A screen in the backseat shows a series of clips and footage. Blood pooled on a walkway. A woman holding her head while blood seeps between her fingers. Body bags being zipped up by people in dark blue windbreakers with guns and badges. A crying child held close by her mother and father. Spent shell casings being removed carefully from the grass and bagged. A man is hit in the head with a brick. A college girl placed in a choke hold. A cop shoved to the ground, pummeled with kicks as the sound of gunfire pops in the background.

An intellectual American voice now joins in. “A lot of people fear this is all far from over. The majority of the futures markets are down across the globe. It’s only Saturday. To be kind, Monday’s open already looks like the Titanic.”

“Amy.” Murphy clears his throat. “Find me some Guns N’ Roses.”

“Yes, Mr. Murphy.”

“Loud, please.”

“Of course, Mr. Murphy.”

“Rocket Queen” rattles the windows. Murphy watches the park as he and Amy roll past. He pulls his phone hoping to see some mindless games to avert his brain. There’s not. Bare bones home screen. No distractions available. He tosses the phone next to him, letting it bounce on the leather.

Can’t help but wonder what special brand of fun awaits in Hell’s Kitchen.

CHAPTER 9

MURPHY WALKS into Johnny Psycho's.

It's the smell of the bar that tugs at Murphy.

Plays with his head as if turning a crank.

Bars have a certain thing. There are smells collected from all the previous nights that hang in the air. They take up residence in the walls and floors. Every bar is slightly different too. Maybe it's the night after night of shepherding men and women in and out, all looking for similar but different things. All in the service of seeking laughs, fun, love or to forget about all of the above.

There's a thing people give off from emotions. It's an animal thing. Subtle, mostly, but if you stuff a pack of those people close together night after night it all starts to accumulate. The constant release of primal human chemicals does something to a space.

Becomes part of it.

Digs into the very foundation.

That and all the booze, vomit and urine over the years have a way of altering the feel of an establishment. Murphy knows bars. Knows them very well. There's a familiarity to the energy of a place like this.

As with most things for him, as he's coming to realize, he feels a sense of knowledge and experience but cannot attach any real memory to that knowledge or experience. Couldn't tell you a story of how or why. No way to access it. No way to tell someone—or himself—where or when he experienced what he thinks he knows. He's never been to Johnny Psycho's, but there's knowledge of this place all the same.

The actual bar area is a visual buffet of good times and bad. A massive mirror has stickers plastered across it. Some old, some new, all decorate the long, tall reflective surface that could use a good cleaning. They announce various bands, brands of booze, and other odd items. Everything from New York college soccer to sex lubricants.

There's no one behind the bar, actually no employees anywhere, but there are four people looking around as if they want a drink. Murphy moves around behind the bar. First day, make a good impression style of thinking.

"Sorry about the wait. What can I get you?" he says to the four.

Scanning them over, he takes in the tats that go up to their necks, and the clothes they wear. This is young money. Tech money he's guessing, considering the young masters of the financial universe have gone the way of the dinosaur in this city. Wall Street ain't what it used to be. Even there, algorithms and tech heads rule the industry.

Small batch, local bourbons and some imported ciders that give the illusion of innovative tastes. Murphy feels good being behind a bar. He works the bottles with ease, hitting the perfect pour on all four glasses of bourbon. He's slipping into a skill he did not understand he had, yet possessed all along. He spreads his fingers along the bar getting the feel of it.

He thinks of his memory. The one that lurks in the back of his jackknifed mind.

The happy man and woman at the bar.

Did I work with the two of them at a bar?

Maybe?

"You Murphy?" a voice thick like gravy asks.

"Yeah." He extends a hand. "Johnny?"

"I am. Get me one of those." Points his chin at the bourbon. "Pour one for yourself too."

Johnny is tall and wide. Long hair with an even longer beard and glasses that resemble Olympic gold rings.

"Not going to argue." Murphy grabs two glasses, giving them both a proper pour.

He slides a glass over to Johnny. They clink them together with a nod then drain them fast. The burn feels amazing to Murphy. Something he's been missing. He's dying to ask Johnny so many questions he doesn't know where to start. This man is the only living source he's got.

"Johnny—"

Johnny puts up a hand, then places a finger to his own lips signaling Murphy not to speak.

"One." Johnny speaks low, looking down trying to hide his lips from whoever might be watching. "I don't know much. And two, I can't tell you a damn thing anyway."

Murphy nods. Understanding, while understanding nothing. His eyes scan the bar while pouring another round. The place is fairly empty. No one stands out to him.

"Oh, and three." Johnny downs his fresh snort. "You're doing the wrong damn job."

"What?"

"Supposed to be working the door."

"What, you mean a bouncer?"

"I do."

"And who wanted that?"

"Friends of yours."

"Same *friends* you won't talk about?"

"Those are the ones." Johnny circles his finger in the air for another round.

Murphy pours while Johnny looks him up and down.

"Gotta say, you don't ooze that standard meaty-boy vibe." Johnny clinks his drink with Murphy's. "No offense. I'm sure you can handle yourself and all that, but dudes who work that shit..." Thumbs toward the red, steel front door. "Those dudes weigh in at three bills and they still take a beating some nights. But hey, that's the shit gig *they* wanted for you, so that, my good man, is the shit gig you shall have."

Johnny Psycho clinks Murphy's glass one last time before walking away.

Murphy stands to the right of the red door.

Arms crossed.

Pissed off.

Johnny gave him a tiny UV LED black light the size of a child's thumb. Was told to use it on IDs to check the patron's validity. It not only verifies the holograms imbedded inside their identification, but also simultaneously scans and feeds the data to servers at Johnny's and the feds. Johnny uses the data for target marketing. He also sells his customers' info to liquor companies, hook-up apps and attorneys who specialize in drunk driving cases and, oh yeah, divorce. Feds use the data for God knows what.

A pack of young, bubbly women bounce up to Murphy.

They make some eyes. Flash their party-proven smiles. Murphy can't help but enjoy it. He flirts a bit, still a human being. Not to mention, Johnny never discussed how much he's being paid, so might as well have a good time. He lets them in. The last one was maybe eighteen. He doesn't care. Johnny sold him out to these *friends* he won't discuss so, ya know, fuck that guy.

Sold to the *they* who will not be named.

His sight blurs.

The pain has come back to say *hello*. He rubs the back of his head. Feels like a cold spike is being wiggled at the base of his skull. Murphy feels his devil face tattoo itch. His teeth grind. The pain eases a bit.

Murphy scans an ID. She turns twenty next month.

"Have a good time." Murphy thumbs her toward the door.

A line is forming. Thirty, maybe forty deep. The music bumps behind him. A mix of current underground beats with cheeky hits from the nineties and early two thousands. The bar is primed and ready. All dolled up for today's drunk and horny to devour. The minutes crawl by. ID after ID passes by his eyes.

Tedious.

Annoying.

Some people bitch and moan. Some are douchebags just because that's who they were born to be. Murphy feels the pain at the base of his skull begin to spread. This door gig is starting to get to him. His shoulders tense, inch up to his ears. Murphy takes a deep breath while he focuses on holding his cold, hard stare. Doesn't want to reveal to the crowd—or to whoever might be watching—the machete that's hacking away at his insides.

He's sure someone has been all over him ever since he's been out here.

Some tough guy with a face tat of a blackbird pushes through to the front of the line. Knocking people aside, he grabs a woman by the arm. Her head whips back as he yanks her toward him.

Murphy clucks his tongue.

As the pain in his skull fades, the itch in his devil face tat shifts into a soothing warmth spreading up his arm and into his chest like the best medicine on earth. Blackbird is the size of a tree. Three times the size of Murphy. Next to him stand two other, even larger dudes. The girl tries to twist away but still manages to put on a fake smile. Her eyes gloss over.

"We're going in." Black Bird shoves Murphy in the chest putting him back on his heels.

A few in line laugh.

"Okay." Murphy scrunches his nose. "Do you have proper identification?"

The line of people collectively hold their breath while talking a step back.

Murphy feels like gears are shifting inside. The three men tower over him. They've got him by several inches and a few hundred pounds. Murphy snickers as if he's in on a joke they're not. He thinks of his gun.

Thinks he won't even need it.

He'll make a bone-crunching show of it. A bloody mess to keep everyone in their proper place. *Hell yeah,* Murphy decides, *prison style this thing.*

No, the voice in back of his mind pleads. *He's not worth it.*

There's a strange confidence. Confidence undeserved yet earned at the same time. Born from having done this in the past with the complete absence of certainty. His mind is a masterclass in leverage and aggression. Tears form. One sole drop begins to roll. He wipes it away fast, checking his fingers. Blood smears across them like red finger paint.

Black Bird shoves Murphy again.

The girl looks disinterested, as if she's seen this routine many times before.

"Asshole." Murphy grinds his teeth, holding back. "You should really get gone."

Light floods the street.

A large SUV screams in from out of nowhere. Tires give a quick squawk as they jump the curb. People scream, scattering in every direction like roaches. Black Bird and his boys run. The brakes slam. Bumper jerks to a stop a few feet from Murphy's knees. Halogen headlights burn high-firing thick beams of light directly into Murphy's face.

There was an SUV in the street last night too.

The doors fly open.

Through the blinding lights Murphy can't see much. Only shapes. Globs of people. Three, maybe more. All holding other, different shapes in their hands.

Armed and moving with extreme purpose toward him.

Murphy whips his Glock free from behind his back. The shadowy figures cut through the bubbling chaos. Murphy feels the blood-tears fall faster.

His devil tattoo aches.

His world tilts.

Vision is swallowed in black.

CHAPTER 10

Murphy's eyes open wide.

Lids flutter like butterfly wings.

Slow to a blink, working... more than a little annoyed by this routine. Firing straight up, he ignores the pain furnace raging from where his spine and skull meet. The bumping throb from his devil tat is reaching unbearable. His chest heaves in and out. A sheen of cold sweat covers his goose skin.

It's getting worse.

It was getting better.

For a little while, at least.

He's feeling all the anxiety now. Every ounce. Wave after wave of unwanted feelings that seemed to have faded are back now with a crippling vengeance—kinda pissed about being ignored. The rational, understandable feelings of terror and dread he had muted are now loud as hell.

Emotions fire in all directions.

He wants to scream.

He wants to be alone. He wants to talk to someone. He wants to cry. Hasn't wanted to do that in... well, never as far as he can recall.

The curtains open.

Sunlight parts the dark. Murphy shields his eyes from the jarring shift in light. Straining, he makes out blobs standing on the other side of the room. Looks to be three of them. The size and shape of them resembles something familiar. Last night. The street in front of the bar. The SUV from last night.

They were coming at him.

They were armed.

Murphy's hand skims under the sheets, under his pillow searching for his gun. His eyes make a quick scan of the bedside table. Empty save for a glass of water and his bottles of pills.

"Missing something?" a man's voice asks in a thick, southern accent.

Even through blurred vision and a gooey mind, Murphy knows the man has his gun. He doesn't recognize the voice, but he knows the accent. More than likely Texan. There's a flattened monophthong even in the two words he spoke. Murphy feels his mind run, accessing a knowledge of language and dialects.

One shape, a man, thick arms and wide shoulders, says nothing as he moves taking a power stance in front of the door. Defense against Murphy making a hasty break for it. This man holds a gun out in plain sight, letting it swing by his side making sure the situation is abundantly clear.

He's big, but big hasn't bothered Murphy so far.

A woman steps into view, along with the man from Texas.

Are they with the muscle boys from the cheap motel?

Were they in the SUV both nights?

More importantly, are they here to kill me?

Away from the direct sunlight, they now stand a few inches from the foot of the bed. She holds a device, a tablet of some sort with a glass screen. The man from Texas is tall. He wiggles Murphy's Glock playfully for Murphy to see then tosses it to the large man guarding the door.

"Do you recognize us?" The man from Texas bites a steel toothpick between his back teeth.

Murphy stares back, not answering. Buying himself time to think. A fool's errand, there's no great move to make here. Fighting to control the rocketing panic is job one at the moment. Murphy knows he's capable of great damage, amazing at producing enormous pain, and wants to do both right now. But still, at this moment he lacks what it takes to access a part of himself that was so dominant.

Murphy's hands shake. He hides them under the sheets.

"No," Murphy finally answers. "Do we know each other?"

The tall Texan grins around his toothpick.

The woman looks Murphy over. Thinks.

"What's the mix?" the Texan asks the woman.

"About 20% Murphy."

"What?" Murphy's face drops.

She studies him then taps and slides her fingers across the glass surface of the tablet. She watches Murphy as warmth spreads out from his forearm. Seemingly coming from the devil face tat, driving up his arm and deep into his chest. A similar fantastic medicine feeling as from the previous nights. An odd minty, antiseptic taste coats his tongue. That's new.

Calm rolls over him.

His breathing slows. His heart slides slightly down from his throat. The sharp pain at the back of his skull pulses, but it is far less than a few seconds ago.

"More like 40% now." She turns to Murphy. "Better?"

Murphy nods.

"I know part of you is considering snapping off various parts of us," the man from Texas says. "Appreciate it if you'd consider reconsidering. Chat with us first?"

"Appreciate you telling me who the hell you are." Murphy's voice cracks. "What do you want?"

"Murphy, going to try and make this brief yet informative." The man from Texas works the toothpick between his teeth. "There's a lot to talk about. Some of it fairly complex, and we have little time to burn while you play catch-up."

The woman seems to be biting her tongue. She bounces on her heels.

The man from Texas looks and talks like a cop. More like a fed. He wears a nice, dark suit with a nice tie. Cost some coin. More than a fed would fork out. It's his shit haircut that's confusing. More importantly, he has those government eyes. The gaze of self-proclaimed badass Murphy recognizes as clear as if he's being reunited with unwanted family. Maybe he's private sector now. Former G-man making some money selling out his past service.

Really wishes he'd stop working that damn steel toothpick with his back teeth.

The woman looks smart.

Academia, maybe.

Could be her glasses coupled with her sharp

business suit that fires off this look of intelligence she's pitching. Hard to trust, under the circumstances. She could be any number of things. Or, it could simply be she is an intelligent person who's also here to gut him like a fish.

"You're safe," she says, tapping the screen again.

You're safe rattles between Murphy's ears.

"Do you believe me?" she asks.

"Is that a joke?" Murphy adjusts the pillows behind his head, getting comfortable. Some of his confidence is back. Feels nice to access this part of himself again. "*Believe you*? No, can't say that I do. Why should I? I don't know you, I—"

"I'm Peyton." She introduces herself with a smile in her voice. There's also a tone. Almost like she's reintroducing herself. "Nothing familiar about me?"

Murphy shakes his head with eyebrows raised high.

"How about me, boss?" The federal dick from Texas holds his arms out wide. "Nothing?"

Murphy starts to say something combative as hell, stops, thinks better of it, then shakes his head.

"He's Thompson," she says. "Formerly, Agent Thompson."

"She's still Dr. Peyton," Thompson adds.

Murphy takes some pride in getting his basic profiling correct.

"You can call me Peyton."

"Tremendous. Again..." Murphy clucks his tongue. "What the hell?"

"Do you remember anything?" Peyton asks. "Anything about your life prior to the last few days?"

"No."

"Okay." She takes in a deep breath, preparing herself. "You may begin to remember things, but for now I'm going to assume you're a blank slate of sorts. I, my company..." Peyton swallows. Resets. "My former company worked in the field of neuroscience. Research. Development. Applying those to real world—"

"Big brain shit," Thompson interjects.

"May I?" Peyton holds a hand up at Thompson. Every word out of him seems to piss her off. "Can I do this?"

"Ticktock, Doctor." Thompson looks to the window. "Why bury the damn lede?"

"Oh? Did you want to do this part?"

"Wouldn't hurt my feelings."

"Could have sworn we discussed this, former Agent Thompson."

"Discussed we'd play it by ear, Dr. Peyton. Said we'd see how things played out."

"After all that's happened, after all that's happening right now, you still—"

"Time's still slipping the hell away. No closer to shoving the genie back in the bottle."

"That's wonderful, truly fantastic," Peyton explodes. "How about you do the easy part, per fucking usual, and I'll handle the big words."

The man guarding the door shifts uneasily.

There's a hard, teeth-rattling silence.

The tension between them seems deeper than people who don't enjoy working together. Murphy can see it. Noticeable how they store stress in every part of their bodies. Maybe they are forced to work together. An unwanted partnership slapped together by a growing, ugly necessity. Mistakes have been made.

Time is an enemy.

These people, they are up against it.

Whatever *it* is.

"Neuroscience, you were saying?" Murphy would rather not *bury the lede* as well.

"Right. I'm going to talk big picture and work down." Peyton clears her throat. Prepares herself again, dagger-eyes at Thompson. "My team, after years of hard work, did what we set out to do—to help people. You probably know this, but most behavioral issues come from various forms of mental illness. Some people have bi-polar or schizophrenia, some are psychopaths. Many suffer from an inability to control their impulses, and those impulses sometimes hurt others."

She looks to Murphy, her eyes wide and warm.

A true believer unspooling her life's work.

"We developed a new method to alter the potentially dangerous, the at-risk people, at a neurological level. We had a team of top-flight researchers, psychologists, brilliant neuroscientists, quantitative masterminds, all creating next generation therapy. We achieved results the psychiatric community could only fantasize about. Truly advanced techniques in helping the disturbed—"

"They figured out how to take deranged fuckers and jam-load non-deranged personalities into their deranged fucker skulls," Thompson cuts in. Couldn't help himself. "In a nutshell." Thompson shrugs, avoiding Peyton's stare, motioning to his wrist—clock is still ticking.

Murphy blinks.

So many questions firing off that he can't pick one to ask.

"What?" he gets out barely above a whisper. "What am I supposed to do with that?"

"Murphy, I know this is unreasonably difficult to understand." Dr. Peyton steps toward him. Thompson puts a hand on her shoulder, gently reminding her to keep a safe distance. "We're about to explain some things and they will seem very strange. I—*we*—understand completely."

"Ever hear about some super-spy shit used back in the '60s?" Thompson stops. Considers. Then.

"Actually, in the '50s if I'm not mistaken. Called MK-Ultra. Mind control stuff? Brainwashing, CIA voodoo shit?"

"Sorry. Missed that class," Murphy says, having trouble focusing.

Thompson looks to Dr. Peyton.

She motions for Thompson to continue.

"Real cloak and dagger shit. Rumors here and there, mixed with some truth, but they were experimenting with a new tactic for the intelligence community to play with."

"In general terms," Dr. Peyton cuts back in, "they imbedded a code into people's brains. Not physical, like a computer chip or anything like that, more reprogramming their minds through intense treatment. Sleep deprivation, along with experimentation with psychoactive drugs. Some illegal surgeries even. So they could—"

"Among other things, place sleeper agents into the general population," Thompson continues. "Strategic locations. Foreign or domestic, to be triggered at any moment. To become cold, hard-hitting folks morally stripped and mentally equipped for murder and mayhem."

Murphy's teeth grind.

Turning away, he sees there's a bottle with two glasses sitting on a bar near the window. Somehow, they knew he enjoyed a pour of whiskey even before he did.

"Any of this landing, Murphy?" Thompson asks.

Murphy gets up from the bed. Dr. Peyton's and Thompson's bodies go tight. They take a step back. The man at the door keeps his eyes locked on him. A finger on the trigger.

"Sixty percent," Peyton says under her breath.

Their fear doesn't go unnoticed by Murphy as he pours two glasses. He pinches the glasses together with his fingers, carrying them in one hand. He picks up the bottle with the other.

"Does this make any sense?" Dr. Peyton asks.

"Understand the words, not sure why you are saying them." Murphy hands one glass to Dr. Peyton, one to Agent Thompson, then takes a slug straight from the bottle.

Dr. Peyton and Thompson trade looks as Murphy walks toward the closet on the other side of the room with bottle in hand. Dr. Peyton moves toward the closet getting closer to Murphy. Thompson hates this. He follows her with a hand on his shoulder holster inside his jacket.

"Murphy," she says.

"Pardon me, good doctor. Getting dressed for my day."

"Ignore me if you want," she says, "but you need to hear this."

Murphy puts on a new shirt, feeling her eyes look him over.

"We, my company, took some findings from the old CIA MK-Ultra program. We integrated those with new ideas based on our own research, adding improved technology, medicine, bleeding-edge psychiatric treatments. We created advanced direct neural overlays. We were able to alter neuropathways using transcranial magnetic stimulation. There was a blend of psychographics, biometrics and AI as well."

"Losing me, Doc."

"Sorry. I need you to know that our work had purpose. Thoughtful purpose. Safe. Humane. Our goal was always to help people."

"Yeah, you said that already."

"I'd like you to understand—"

"Fine. You're an amazing, caring person."

"Please—"

"Doc? Peyton, is it?" Murphy says. "You do brains, and my brain is warm garbage. Please, let us step away from the bullshit, and explain what the hell happened to me."

Her eyes close. Wounds still fresh and tender.

"I promise this is relevant. We had higher goals of working with the overcrowding prisons. Trying to help youth struggling with social and legal issues stemming from childhood abuse. Trying to help the mentally ill." Murphy can hear her passion for her work. "It was all a new, radical form of therapy. Helping heavily burdened minds shift to a better state. A better place for the patient and for society. There are endless applications. Possible relief for people struggling with all kinds of neurological issues. What if we could cure Parkinson's by overlaying damaged neurons?"

Peyton looks to Thompson.

Even the hard-ass Thompson is moved by the emotion behind her words.

Silently she mouths, *tell him.*

Murphy steps out from the closet. He's changed into gray jeans, a black T-shirt and some high-dollar sneakers. He likes this new uniform he's recently adopted. Murphy stands looking at them, waiting, not sure where this is going and not sure he wants to know. He rubs the devil tattoo on the inside of his forearm. Looks much better. The clear film has been removed.

Thompson clears his throat. "And that, right or wrong, is where you come in."

"Yes, please, between the two of you, locate the damn point," Murphy says.

"Markus Murphy. Decorated Marine. Quickly caught the eye of some big, important folks who thought you'd be a good fit for their dirty deeds." Thompson drinks from the glass of whiskey Murphy gave him. Makes an approval face. *The good stuff.* "Unfortunately, you're also someone who played a little fast and loose. By fast and loose I mean violent and psycho. A remarkably skilled killer, but psychotic, nonetheless. You were locked up at the USDB in Leavenworth. Doing life, sadly."

Murphy hears the information but has no recall.

He doesn't fight it either.

Everything Thompson says feels like it makes sense even though he can't see a single frame of it play in his mind. His words ring true as any known fact would. Statements that cannot be argued.

It makes another part of Murphy want to throw up.

"You were the perfect test subject." Thompson smiles.

"*Perfect*? Flattering as hell." Murphy taps his finger against his lips, mocking Thompson. "Could have sworn I heard something about this kindly woman digging in my skull."

"You signed up for this." Thompson shrugs.

"Going to need more than that," Murphy says, moving in fast.

Thompson places a hand on his gun again.

The large man guarding the door clears his throat, adjusting his grip on his weapon.

"Hovering around 70%," Dr. Peyton says, waving them off. "We had completed some early trials. Done well with some test subjects—easier subjects. Fewer psychological issues to sort out than you."

"Touching." Murphy takes a swig from the bottle, pushing past them toward the door.

"You were the perfect benchmark." Dr. Peyton speeds up. They're losing him. "We knew if we could help you, if we could make you good—for lack of a better term—then we knew we had reached the top of the mountain. You were on death row. It was a chance to live longer."

"So what went wrong, big brains?" Murphy steps toward the man blocking the door.

"What makes you think anything went wrong?" Thompson asks.

"Well, my memory is shit, you seem slightly on edge, and—oh yeah—why the hell would anyone release someone as dangerous as I apparently am out into the world?" He gestures around the room. "Shouldn't I be chained up in a lab? So, one more time with feeling, what the hell went wrong?"

"With all major scientific studies, funds are needed and lots of it," Peyton says. "We were well into our work when the money dried up. That's when they approached us."

"Who's *they*? Wait. I'll take a stab." Murphy resets. "Guessing the same organization ass-bucket here works for." Murphy pushes his chin toward the man guarding the door.

"If *ass-bucket* means valued CIA employee, then you are correct," Thompson jumps in. "The CIA funds many entrepreneurial endeavors ranging from tech to medical. Unlimited funding with strings they don't bother mentioning."

"You're no scientist. She said *former agent.* So..." Murphy looks Thompson over. "Guessing that makes you a former ass-bucket—current dick-head—and you made the introduction between the ass-buckets and the genius, big brain, mind benders."

Thompson nods, setting his drink down.

"They told us they'd be hands off," Dr. Peyton says.

"They lied," Thompson adds.

"They do that." Murphy turns back to the man guarding the door.

"Necessity made us stupid. They told us what we wanted to hear." Dr. Peyton stands next to Thompson. "They had their own team of scientists. Teams of everything. They took our work, our processes and worked on their own agenda. They took our research without our knowledge and worked in a separate location. They did sloppy work."

"They did the opposite of Dr. Peyton." Thompson looks Murphy up and down trying to get a read on him. "Instead of taking a killer and making him nice, they took nice folk and mixed them up in a blender with a psychopath."

"Wait. Other people are going through this?" Sadness creeps into Murphy. Compassion he couldn't imagine accessing not long ago. "Why?" Murphy blinks away the unsolicited emotion.

"They wanted, much like the old MK-Ultra days, assets crafted in a lab that could be perfectly placed and unleashed," Thompson says. "Better than any field agent. These people would be truly undercover. Even from themselves. They wanted—"

"On-demand killers," Murphy says.

He lets his own words hover in the air.

Peyton looks him over, thinks, then taps the screen of her tablet.

Murphy's tattoo tingles, and a moment later his eyes light up. A mental reset.

"Great. Really fun." Murphy claps his hands loudly, blowing up this moment of thoughtful reflection. "So, you overlaid some Mr. Nice Guy neural pathways with my badass brain?"

Dr. Peyton nods.

"Super neat." Murphy looks around. "Still, why are we here?"

Peyton looks away. Doesn't want to tell him.

Even Thompson looks to his shoes.

"What? Who farted?" Murphy asks.

Big silence.

"Spill it, kids. What don't you want to tell me?"

"There's been a problem." Peyton's voice breaks.

"Big one," Thompson adds.

"The people the CIA worked on have escaped." Peyton looks down. "They're out loose in the world, and we can't find them."

"And Murphy?" Thompson sighs. "The side they used to blend with these people. The bad side? The psychopath? That's 100% the old you, buddy."

CHAPTER 11

"You're the alpha," Thompson says.

Murphy feels himself peel away.

Floating, no longer a part of the room.

He wants to remove the urge to feel anything. Become untethered from himself. Wants to be anyone but what they say he is. Guilt hits him like a sledgehammer. Not sure why, he did nothing wrong. Still, he fights feeling responsible no matter how unreasonable that might be.

The whiskey burns the good burn as he takes a cleansing a pull from the bottle.

Dr. Peyton talks to him.

So does Thompson.

Their lips visibly move, but Murphy cannot connect any of the words to their source. The sounds of their voices enter his ears, but they only skim the perimeter of his thoughts. Their tone, the words, buzzes like flies around rotting meat.

Thompson places one hand on each of Murphy's shoulders.

Murphy slaps them away, landing a flat palm into Thompson's chest like a battering ram. Thompson stumbles back, bounces off the wall raising his hands in a peaceful gesture. Murphy considers dropping him to the floor. Takes a swig from the bottle instead.

The man guarding the door raises his weapon.

Murphy smiles, wagging his finger at him like a child who's spilled some juice. Murphy's feeling himself come back to the room. Shaken free from the haze. His mind sharpens.

He's back online.

"Murphy, we need you." Dr. Peyton moves closer. Her words now landing. "You are the only one who knows these people better than we do. They are part you. Please, will you help us find these people?"

"I need you to get all the way off my back with that *help us* shit." Murphy stares hard into the eyes of the man guarding the door. Murphy can taste the man's fear. "Also need you to move away from that door, my man."

"You with us?" Thompson asks. "Or against us?"

Murphy wants to run. No idea where to but anywhere but here.

"This can get damn ugly, damn fast,"

Thompson says, "but it doesn't have to. We can offer you things. More like we can offer you everything."

Dr. Peyton never takes her eyes off Murphy.

She's studying everything he does. Murphy breathes in deep through his nose, exhaling long and steady through his lips. Maintaining a loose grip on control. His appetite for bloodshed rising by the second. That voice is back. The annoying spectator calling out at the back of a room. A lone voice of reason begging for a better solution.

"They're out there." Peyton tries to talk him down. "We're not even sure how many."

"We've got a lead on one of them." Thompson keeps his hand on his gun.

"Moo-ove," Murphy singsongs to the man guarding the door. Cocks his head. "Do I have to count?"

The man steps back, leveling his weapon on Murphy's face.

"Really, guy?" Murphy scrunches his nose. "I have to count, right?"

"Murphy, there's something else you need to know," Peyton says.

"Oh, I'm sure." Leaning in, Murphy places his forehead on the barrel of the gun. "One..."

The guard's eyes bounce to Thompson then back to Murphy.

"Love it if you just said you wanted to help out.

Be cleaner. Easier," Thompson says. "We both know you can take that gun away from him."

"Only want mine back." Murphy clucks his tongue. "Two..."

"Pretty sure you've already thought up three ways to kill all of us."

"Four, actually, and a fifth is looking pretty cool."

"Ya know that pain you have in the back of your skull?" Thompson asks. "Remember what happened when you tried to leave the room last time?"

Murphy stops cold.

"Yeah, you know what I'm talking about. That pain? It ain't stress or some seasonal sinus thing."

Dr. Peyton now drinks her first sip of whiskey.

"You complete piece of shit." Murphy's knuckles pop. "What did you do to me?"

"Look, you can keep counting. You can snap this big boy's neck, then kill me and kill Dr. Peyton any way you please. But if you walk out that door?" Thompson locks eyes with Murphy. "You're going to die."

"Well then." Murphy keeps his head on the barrel of the gun, rolling, tilting his face toward Thompson. "Listening ears are on."

Thompson grins. "It's real simple."

Murphy twists the gun away from the guard. Flicks it across the room, then cracks him over the head with the whiskey bottle. In a single move, Murphy pulls his Glock away from the guard's belt before his body hits the carpet.

Light on the sights turns green.

"New plan." Murphy presses the barrel between Thompson's eyes. "Dr. Peyton and I have a drink downstairs. She seems slightly less full of shit than you. Besides..."

He nods toward the bottle spilling whiskey into the guard's face.

"This room sucks now."

CHAPTER 12

THE HOTEL BAR is a monument to money and those with money who enjoy the drink.

Light bounces off the endless hanging glass and chrome that stretches up to an unseen ceiling somewhere in heaven. The aggressively attractive staff is dressed in black tie no matter the day or the time. A picture window frames a normally gorgeous view of the park. Today, it shows the picture of growing unrest outside the hotel.

Dr. Peyton and Murphy sit at a large, circular booth fit for six.

Murphy picked a spot in the white leather across from her. One that's far enough away for her to feel comfortable, but still close enough to be heard over the smooth electronic ambient beats cascading from unseen sources.

Whiffs of sizzling steak drift in from the restaurant just off the bar. The smells draw him back.

Not sure to what, but the sights, sounds and smells do take him to a better place.

Toward happiness, even.

The waitress jolts him out from his thoughts, dropping off two whiskeys—neat.

Murphy didn't bother telling her what brand, only requesting the most expensive the bar has to offer. He doesn't particularly care. Murphy isn't completely sure if he enjoys the high-end or the cheap stuff. This is more about the size of the bill that's headed toward the Texan sitting at the bar. He waves to Thompson and the large man who once bravely guarded the hotel room's door, but now sits with his pulsing head wrapped in a bar towel full of ice.

"Thompson is an impossible human being, no question," Dr. Peyton says. "But with you, he's being an asshole on purpose."

"Adorable."

"All of this is part of testing you. All of it. Seeing how you perform out in the real world. Seeing how you responded at the run-down motel room, contrasting that with this high-end hotel, and also your interactions while working at that bar. Studying how you reacted to Thompson pushing your buttons. Monitoring those reactions. These are the things we cannot replicate in a lab. Part of you responds to things differently than the other side of you."

"You enjoying this? Because I'm not."

"Thompson's right." Dr. Peyton takes a sip, keeping her eyes on Murphy. Uneasiness noticeably present. "We don't really have time to burn. Like an answer from you."

Are you with us?

Like he has a choice.

"Let's make the words count then. I have a few questions, as you might imagine." Murphy downs his glass. Circles a finger for more. "There's the umbrella topic of *what the fuck*, but we'll put a pin in that one. Let's start with a softball. What the hell did he mean by I was *going to die* if I walked out the door?"

"Okay." She takes another sip, chooses her words. "We were in the final stages with you, before the escape, a stage that was meant to last weeks, perhaps months, but definitely not days."

Murphy softly taps his finger on the wood of the table.

Patience fading.

Stabbing stare.

"Like I said, we didn't know what you'd do out in the world, okay? Thompson called it *releasing a grizzly into an orphanage.* And to be perfectly honest, you didn't do so great in the early tests. So..." She sips again. "We installed a fail-safe of sorts."

"And that is?"

The waitress drops off a new drink for Murphy.

"There's a small, microscopic device installed at the base of your skull. Advanced nanotech detonation tech that can be activated if we ever—"

"Need to blast out the back of my head." Murphy downs the second drink and circles for a third. "If or when I become an unnecessary evil."

She nods.

"Sweet baby balls," Murphy says.

"Such a bad idea putting whiskey in the room." Dr. Peyton shakes her head. "Thompson's, for the record."

"Best idea he's ever had." Murphy shifts gears. "How did they get my brain? How does that happen? I mean how'd the big bad CIA get me into the ones that escaped?"

"Not as simple as uploading one personality to another." She considers, then motions for another drink as well. "It's more than complicated."

"Talk to me like I'm five then."

"Like I said before, we instituted a remapping of neural pathways."

"Give me the protein, Doc."

"We had access to your files." She looks for the new drink to arrive "To the *work* you did in the military and the CIA. Detailed accounts of everything so we would know what questions to ask you. Where to dig."

"Okay."

"So, we interviewed you. We did it to understand you better. See how a troubled mind truly works. We recorded you talking about what you were thinking during the things you did. About how killing made you feel. How you mentally processed the pain you inflicted on people. Managing a void where remorse and morality would normally reside." She takes the glass from the waitress, downing it much like Murphy. "Carefully curated, layered, psychological questions. Hours, perhaps days' worth of your mind spilled out for us to examine. Careful, detailed questions you answered while we mapped your neural pathways." She takes a breath. "The *protein*, as you say, is highly advanced, targeted medication coupled with sleep deprivation, constant repetition of your thoughts *layered,* for lack of a better term through—"

"That brain magnet pathway shit?"

"Transcranial magnetic stimulation. TCMS. I can't speak to what the CIA did exactly, but using the data we had from you, all of those processes performed in the right order, in the right way, can create an intentional, purposeful dissociative identity."

"Custom-built split personality."

"The science is dense, but yes, something like that."

Murphy's eyes glaze. Retreating into himself as the information floods his brain. One singular question swims to the surface.

"Who am I split with?"

Peyton looks away.

Murphy slams his hands down on the table. Loud. Hard. Their glasses jump, bouncing a splatter of whiskey onto the table. Murphy playfully bounces his eyebrows then places a finger to his head, raising his thumb like a gun.

"Who the hell is in here?"

Thompson stands up from the bar placing one hand on the sidearm inside his jacket.

Dr. Peyton motions for him to stand down. She's got this—hopefully.

Murphy snaps his fingers, bringing her attention back to their chat.

"Got to be someone." He thumps his thumbs on the table in a quick drumbeat. "I don't remember much about myself, or much of anything actually. But there are times where I can almost hear how different my thoughts are." Murphy's eyes shift to Thompson then back to her. "Who's joined this little skull party of mine? Seems like a really nice guy."

Murphy sees her hand move to her tablet.

As the tips of her fingers glide along the glass, his emotions tilt. A shift in what's living under his skin. Accessible anger replaced by resident fear.

Confidence overrun by a stampede of question and doubt. He locks his fingers tightly in front of him to control the shaking.

His eyes are full.

Open wide.

Mr. Nice Guy is now speaking for Murphy.

"I can't remember anything, Dr. Peyton. Nothing. Nothing about my life, family, friends..." His chin quivers. He clears his throat. "Most of time I'm terrified. Terrified of the world. Of, well, of me honestly." Murphy gathers himself, sits up straight. "Please. Tell me something."

"I... We..." She starts, then stops. Thinks. Then starts again. "I'm sorry, I am, but there are things I can't share. Not right now. They're unproductive. Harmful to you even."

"I have the right." Murphy feels himself tilt the other way again.

Shoving Mr. Nice Guy aside.

Murphy locks eyes. Tired of the bullshit.

Peyton watches him turn. She reaches for the tablet.

"Stop." Murphy's tone cuts like an ice-cold blade. "Whatever you're about to do, do not. As you've clearly stated, part of me has progressive views on violence."

Peyton pulls her hand back from the screen.

"Your mind is a work in progress. There's psychologic trauma you haven't been allowed to deal with." She gestures to her tablet. "I use this device to attempt to even out the chemical reactions in your brain. As we *test* you, I make updates, tweaks here and there as your new neural pathways reconcile. The mix with you is tricky. The balancing act is difficult, to say the least. We tried to do this all at once before, just last week, and we nearly fried your brain."

"Sorry to be so difficult to work with." His hands press harder and harder into the table.

"Our process takes time. Time we haven't been allowed. Events have forced us to where we are now. You understand? You've had no chance to heal. Our recovery schedule was negated. Obliterated. No opportunity for us to study results."

"You treated my brain like a truck stop bathroom, then you pitch me some lofty bullshit about saving society via a science fair project. Now, you're threatening to light up my brain if I don't fix the fucked-up shit you never should have fucked up in the first place."

She bites the inside of her cheek. Concern mounting. She looks to her tablet.

"Murphy, I'm sorry this has happened to you. But I need you to try and understand."

"Need you to eat shit."

"The treatments need a chance to run their course. The changes in you will stabilize. Your thoughts, your memory will eventually even out."

"When?"

"I don't know. Days, weeks, maybe months."

"Or never."

Peyton stares at him blankly. No response to give.

Murphy's shoulders inch up. It's as if he's watching himself engaged in this insane conversation. It's impossible to hear you're mixing minds with anyone, let alone with a killer absent of remorse.

Dr. Peyton's hands wrap tightly around her whiskey glass. Her jaw sets. Her eyes dance.

It hits Murphy like a freight train.

"You heard them. The questions? The answers I gave?"

"I was in the room, for all of it."

"Are you..." Murphy's voice breaks, already knowing the answer. "Are you scared of me?"

"Murphy..." She takes a drink. "You terrify me."

Murphy, without thinking, reaches out to hold her shaking hand. Looking to comfort himself as much as her. Peyton pulls her hand back fast, as if his fingers were on fire. Her face is frozen in fear. Murphy raises his hands off the table, leans back showing he meant no harm.

He hates the look in her eyes.

The intense fear she's experiencing.

He wants to explain that he's not what they think he is. Even if he knows...

She should be afraid.

They have forced his poisoned mind onto others. Men and women have been forever removed from normal lives, altered to be like Murphy.

A killer.

A mass murderer.

Images of the violence he's waged stream inside his mind. The street in New York. The searing urge to let bodies drop in front of the bar's door. All of it plays out like a movie ripping at 3x speed.

Something else occurs to him. The few memories he's been able to see. The lifeless bodies, the blood at the house by the water. The gun in his hand. The stillness, the calm he displayed standing among the dead. The older woman screaming. All vivid as hell.

Excruciating to know you are that kind of monster.

Then, with the same level of clarity, there's a single snap of happiness. A memory that glows, provides a smile to his broken, beaten mind. The single scene of the man and woman at the bar rushes back to him like a stampede.

"I lied. I do remember." Murphy leans forward on the table. "Nothing much. Usually when I'm asleep, but sometimes not."

"Okay." She leans in. Energized by the possibility of his words. "Like what?"

"Feels like memories, but... off. Fuzzy. There's two, I think. One feels like it's me, but there's one that's different." He cracks a small smile. "I'm a spectator. Watching other people. There's a man and a woman at a bar. They're laughing, really enjoying each other, you know? It's only a few seconds or so, but it's so clear. Alive."

"Oh my God." Dr. Peyton's face drops.

He's hit on something. Murphy has her complete attention.

She wants to know everything going on in his splintered mind. She has just as many—maybe more—questions as he does.

He *is* her life's work.

A living, breathing embodiment of everything she's worked and sacrificed to achieve. This is his chance. His currency. He has something to trade to get answers by leveraging her passion. He returns to the big question that still picks at him.

"Whose life did you feed into me?"

"Murphy—"

"Who?"

"I can't."

"Okay." He takes a sip, then places his palms flat on the table. "I'm not telling you a damn thing about my broken brain."

Peyton's fingers tap a nervous rhythm on the

table. Her head nods ever so slightly. Murphy imagines her knee working overtime under the table. Up and down like a jackhammer. It's killing her. She has so many things she wants to know, and all she has to do is talk.

"You give." Murphy leans in. "I give."

Peyton wilts. Her shoulders drop.

"An ordinary guy in an unfortunate situation."

A spike of anger jolts Murphy. He cocks his head.

Peyton holds up a hand, asking for a moment. She exhales big.

"He was a fit for what we needed. Unfortunately, he was brought in moments before he passed away. We were able to map his strongest thoughts before he died."

"Wow. You're right, Dr. Peyton. You are a good person." Murphy leans back. "You snatched a person's dying thoughts right out of his head, didn't you?"

"There was nothing we could do for him. His injuries were too severe. He indicated that he wanted his body to be used for—"

"I... He checked a box on his driver's license so you backdoored that into—"

"Do you want to know or not?"

Murphy stares back at her, then nods a yes.

"We analyzed emails, texts, social media posts, pictures, videos. The music he liked, favorite movies and books. Purchasing habits and patterns. There were dozens of voicemails we found. Analyzed where he grew up, where he went to school, jobs he's had. Everything we could find about his family. All of it was used to create an artificial, yet extremely accurate, depiction of a person. We fed that data into our advanced quant models. Then, our algorithms linked together a psychological mock-up that filled in any gaps."

"You've got to be shitting me." Murphy takes a beat. Takes a drink. "You stitched together a human being? A reconstructed personality you force-fed into me?"

"It's complicated."

"Yeah, you said that."

"Look. We can take turns punching each other in the face, but—"

"Was *he* a good person?" Heart sinks even asking the question. Murphy can feel Mr. Nice Guy inside his head. "Is he better than me?"

"He was. That was the whole point of this project. Healthy minds helping unhealthy."

Murphy looks away. Her directness cuts him to the bone.

"He is you. In a way."

"Mr. Nice Guy have a name?"

"I can't tell you. Only further complicates your thoughts. Creates more separation."

"What happened to him?"

"Car accident. Drunk driver."

A vision of a spinning, flipping car flashes in Murphy's mind. The terror. The sounds. The pain. He remains stone-faced, staring at her from across the table. Not wanting to give her anything.

"That's all I can say. Probably said way too much." Dr. Peyton thinks of taking another drink but pushes the glass away from her.

Murphy absorbs the weight of the conversation.

Dr. Peyton raises her eyebrows, waiting for her turn to ask questions. Murphy holds the moment. His only moment of power in this world. He fights the urge to ask more. Hates it, but he realizes he might have to accept this as progress—for now.

He nods for her to have her turn.

"That night, the first one, at the dingy motel," she asks, "did you see things?"

"Yeah, saw some big bastards trying to kill me."

"Okay." Huge smile. There's a vibrating excitement in her eyes as she taps feverishly on her tablet. "Okay. What does my face look like?"

"What? What the hell are you—" His expression drops.

Dr. Peyton's face morphs into that of a demon. Eyes that burn white. Skin turns the color of the darkest red wine, then bubbles as if cooking on the bone. Similar to what he saw that night.

"What did you do?"

"There." She points to his devil tat. "Surgical implant. Through that I can control various chemicals inside your mind. Don't remove it, by the way. You'll bleed out in like forty-two seconds."

Murphy fumbles for the right question as her face fades back into its normal state.

"Nobody chased you that night," she says. "You were hallucinating. That was the first test. A safer test to create a baseline for us to work from. You didn't actually hurt anyone, but that's not the point. You reacted purely on impulse. Your impulses are to kill first, talk later."

"Okay." An odd sense of relief. Then... "So wait, the bar was real?"

"It was. You didn't almost kill anybody there, so that was progress. Like I said, balance is tricky with you. We appreciate your violence, but only measured and when appropriate," she says as if talking to herself but looking directly him. "Did one night feel different from the other?"

"Maybe. I don't know. It's different each time." Murphy's mind swims. "Everything becomes heightened. Like riding an escalator going up so fast it's hard to process. Headed to a place you don't want to go. Other times, it's not like that at all. It feels—I don't know—liberating?"

"We done?" A pissed off Thompson now stands by the table. "We need to move."

"This is fascinating. Truly." Peyton's eyes

dance. "There's so much to learn. His mind is viewing memories as a third party—"

"Wonderful." Thompson motions for the check. "Lady Brubaker is in play."

"Shit." All color drains from Peyton's face.

"Who?" Murphy asks.

"We have to go now." Peyton grabs her tablet, rushing out from the booth.

Murphy's fingers press into the table, still seeking that illusive calm in the storm.

"Murphy?" Thompson does some piss-poor jazz hands. "Happy hour is over."

CHAPTER 13

"HERE'S WHAT WE HAVE."

Dr. Peyton reaches back, handing Murphy a tablet encased in a synthetic, everything-proof cover. Thompson cuts through the traffic clutter with a casual focus. Driving at a rate of speed reserved for people who know laws do not apply. The city races by the tinted glass in a gray smear of architecture and people.

Dr. Peyton rides shotgun, with Murphy bouncing and swaying in the back seat. He grips the *oh shit* handle, his gun next to him about an inch from his thigh. The SUV smells like government. Murphy can feel the bureaucracy coat his skin.

It's too clean. Too beige. Too little to like or enjoy.

What the agency would consider luxury, Murphy thinks.

"Before we get to that, another thing's puzzling me." Murphy clears his throat. "Why the hell do I bleed from my eyes?"

Peyton turns around. "Is that happening?"

"Love for it to stop."

"Okay." She thinks. "That's haemolacria. It should subside soon. Don't worry. It's a side effect. Usually seen with brain tumors or—"

"Gutting my mind?"

"Something like that."

"Can we get back to the problem at hand?" Thompson cuts in. "That would be wonderful."

"Please, sugar bear," Murphy says. "Contribute."

"There's a woman they call Lady Brubaker." Thompson punches the pedal down, checking the mirrors constantly. "We think she's the leader."

"She is the leader," Peyton corrects him. "Watch the security video we pulled from the escape."

"Not much to learn there. Only nightmares in the making." Thompson lays down the horn, jerks the wheel hard, then jams on the gas. "Hell, take a look. You'll see."

Murphy looks to Dr. Peyton. She only offers a stare in return. He takes a deep breath, thinking that whatever is beyond the glass screen is the beginning, or the end, of his life.

Whatever *his life* may mean.

Murphy taps the fat white arrow.

The screen lights up an ultra-clear 5K video shot from a raised security camera. So clear it doesn't look like real life. It overlooks what could best be described as a garden-variety lab. Off-white walls with a concrete floor littered with gleaming steel tables and chairs. There's a small grouping of men and women in light blue lab coats with their hands raised. They are backing up toward a closed door behind them.

Their eyes are focused dead ahead.

Two of them hold guns in unsteady hands. Not comfortable with the weapons they hold, but still have them pointed at a threat just out of the camera's eye.

Hard to make out what's being said. A jumbled chaos of sound, difficult to single out words. Hard to parse any tangible sentence. The city sounds from outside the SUV aren't helping either. Regardless, there's no question their screaming is born from fear. Pleading for this to stop. For mercy. Their expressions are hard. Faces red. Their heads turn back and forth toward the door. Panicked looks traded between them. One has his hand on the door handle behind him. Moving slow as if not to be noticed. Noticed by whoever is generating all this fear just out of the camera's view.

Someone moves into frame.

Shoved is more accurate.

There's a man being held with a knife to his throat. The face of the person holding the knife is still offscreen, but the hand is small. The arm is thin, but muscular and covered in tattoos. There's sudden silence. Noise ends. Everyone stops screaming, standing motionless, waiting.

A single voice screams out, "No!"

Several look away.

The man's throat is cut. He falls forward to the tile floor with red spilling out from him.

A woman steps into frame.

A woman with raven hair highlighted with tips kissed with purple. She stands over the body holding a bloody knife then turns, looking up directly into the security camera. Staring at the audience she knows is watching or will be soon enough. She holds her piercing gaze, as if staring out from the glass of the tablet.

Her stare carves through Murphy.

She holds her knife above her head, circling it in the air.

A crowd rushes out from behind her. Passes by the raven-haired woman as if she's a stationary stone in a raging river. Armed with miscellaneous items, probably from the lab. A few hold surgical knives. Some wield pipes or table legs with jagged edges from where they were torn away. Most storm in with only wild eyes and hands bare. Zero fear of the guns in front of them.

Shots fire.

One of them drops.

Another pauses, for only a blink, absorbs the bullet, then keeps running toward the people in lab coats. The men and women spin, reaching for the door. Overrun before they can pull it open. Sounds of brutality test the tablet's speakers. The attack is primal. Animalistic. Screams are cut short. Bones crunch. The sound of tearing flesh is clear even through tiny speakers. Murphy watches on, feeling the tug of war inside of him.

Part horrified.

Part impressed.

The woman, Lady Brubaker he assumes, stands perfectly still. Her eyes focused on the security camera. She never looks away, not once, not even as the shots fired. A man with his face decorated with sprays of blood hands her a gun. Lady Brubaker takes it, smiles, then gives the camera the finger.

Her gaze is like a funeral.

She fires the gun.

The screen goes blank.

Murphy exhales.

He sets the tablet down next to his gun then cracks open a water bottle that was sitting in the car door. The world blazes by the window as Thompson continues carving up the city in pursuit of an unknown location.

"They're like this..." Murphy swallows.

"They're like this because they've been changed to be like me?"

Peyton glances back at Murphy. A mix of warmth and concern.

"When did this happen?" Murphy asks, shaking it off.

"We got it not long after you woke up in the first motel," Peyton says.

"Good news is..." Thompson jams the breaks, then punches it again. "We've got eyes on Lady Brubaker as we speak and—"

"Then send in a team and take her out," Murphy barks. "What the hell do you want me to do with this?"

"Don't you think we tried that?" Thompson looks at him through the rearview mirror.

"We found her along with a handful of the others," Dr. Peyton adds. "We sent in a team, like you said, and—"

"Lady Brubaker and her friends slaughtered them." Thompson puts a period on the conversation. "All of them. An entire tactical team of highly trained badasses were eliminated in minutes. Those monsters carved through them like they were nothing. Then they disappeared into the wind."

"Until now." Dr. Peyton turns back to Murphy. "She's been spotted."

"How many are out there?" Murphy asks.

"Not completely sure," Dr. Peyton says. Thompson begins to speak, but Dr. Peyton stops him. "Best we can tell, from the video you saw and other sources, there are at least seven out in the wild. Eight counting Brubaker. One died in the escape, another was wounded, but we don't know exactly how many—"

"And you want me to do what?" Murphy asks. "Hunt them down? Kill 'em all?"

"Would you mind?" Thompson can't help himself.

"No," Peyton barks at Thompson. Resets, then turns back to Murphy. "That's the last resort. We'd like to have all of them back alive, but even I realize that's unrealistic given what we've seen. In your bag are multiple doses of a powerful sedative. We have loaded them into small injectors, size of a dime, but work as fast as a hypodermic. If you can get close enough, you can inject anywhere on their body and walk away."

"We'll clean up the mess," Thompson says, "but make no mistake. Lethal force is completely authorized."

"You don't say." Murphy closes his eyes.

"Encouraged, actually."

"And if I don't? If I'd rather not? You what?" Murphy asks. "You kill me? That the pitch?"

"That's the fine print, yes." Thompson doesn't bother glancing in the rearview.

"You'll have us." Peyton tries to smooth things out. "We have access to some agent support. Not as much as we'd like, but some."

"Considering the off-the-books nature of this," Thompson adds.

"But we do have people," Peyton says, firing eye-daggers at him.

"Impressive."

"Look, man." Thompson stares back. "You don't have a whole helluva lot of leverage."

Murphy raises his gun.

"What if I pop both of you?" Murphy looks to Dr. Peyton. "Seems there's not a lot of folks that know about me. Most of the ones who did are already dead. I'm guessing anyone else out there either doesn't know, doesn't want to know, or they're willing to deny they had any knowledge of this shitshow."

"Murphy. Don't," Dr. Peyton pleads.

Dr. Peyton readies her tablet.

"Now, now." Murphy presses the barrel to her head. "Don't go tapping my mind into submission."

"I'm not." She turns the screen slowly to face him. "You need to see this."

On screen is a simple application. A clock that is counting down. Ticking down one second at a time, thirty-five seconds left before reaching zero. At the bottom are a red button and a green one.

Childlike simplicity.

"This is tied to what's been placed at the base of your skull. It has a signal to a satellite, along with everything else going on inside you." Dr. Peyton's tone is ice-cold. More chilling than Murphy's witnessed from her. "It must be reset every day. Bio-recognition. We both have to check in once a day via a retinal eye scan. If we don't—"

"Murphy's brain goes boom-boom."

"You're fun." Murphy grinds.

"When this is over, when the situation is secure." Dr. Peyton holds her finger over the red button. "And when we feel you've balanced out psychologically—"

"You mean control me."

"Yes," Dr. Peyton continues. "That is exactly correct."

Murphy removes his gun from Peyton's face. He was fairly sure that would not work, but he felt he had to touch all the bases. Due diligence is always a good idea when dealing with people who are trying to get you killed. Murphy sets his gun back down on the seat beside him.

He hears a woman's voice say something.

A single sentence plays inside his head.

You're like a playground wrapped in barbed wire.

The voice is soft and kind, but Murphy doesn't recognize the sound of her. Her tone is familiar, someone who knows or knew him. Whatever *him* means now. This combination of Murphy and Mr. Nice Guy. Seems like the woman's voice is part of his past that he can't put in a proper file.

"You okay?" Peyton asks.

Murphy waves her off.

On the floorboard is the metal suitcase from the hotel room. Popping it open, he sees that his clothes have been packed up nice and neat, along with his medications, a rubber band-bound roll of cash, and what he assumes are the dime-sized injectors Dr. Peyton was yammering about.

"You'll have a few more things in the car," Thompson says, pushing down the pedal.

Murphy hadn't even noticed they'd reached the highway.

"Car?" Murphy asks.

CHAPTER 14

"WHAT A HUNK OF SHIT," Murphy says.

He, Dr. Peyton and Thompson stare into an open trunk that stinks of death and lost hope. Rusted holes decorate the bottom with various fast-food wrappers scattered about. Murphy has his gun tucked in the waist of his jeans with his T-shirt covering it. He holds the tablet Peyton gave him in one hand, suitcase in the other.

Thompson peels back what's left of the trunk's lining.

A silver trash bag is lumped inside the hole where the spare would normally live. Thompson holds his hand out inviting Murphy to give it a look.

"Presents?" Murphy asks.

"Your troubled past has been erased," Peyton says. "The best we could at least."

"What do you mean?" Murphy asks.

"She means all the terrible you've inflicted has been forgiven. All the shit out there about the horrific human being you truly are has been removed. A new profile has been spread out over the world. You may have noticed the car you jumped into at the hotel knew you."

"Nicer car than this," Murphy adds.

"We wanted to reset your footprint as much as we could. Tax records, the little you had, are gone. Fingerprint recognition, face identification, retinal scans have all been fitted with a new version of you."

"And that is?"

"One that doesn't murder everything moving," Thompson says.

Murphy turns his attention back to the trunk.

Inside the bag are stacks of cash in various currencies, along with a clear plastic bag that contains what looks like are different forms of ID. Most are under the name Markus Murphy. There are also several fake driver's licenses clipped to fake passports, with real credit cards that match the crap names on the IDs. There's also another Glock, fully loaded magazines, spare boxes of high-velocity rounds, a classic .38 Special with an ankle holster and a tactical knife. A cold, clean blade made of military-grade steel. There are also three high-end black ski masks. Murphy's best guess is he needs three in case the first two get soiled with blood and/or brain matter.

Thompson hands Murphy the fob to the forgettable 2017 Japanese sedan.

"Really?" Murphy asks. "Masters of the dark arts couldn't get wheels from this decade?"

"Needed something nondescript." Thompson fights a laugh. "Can't have a five-star psycho roaming the countryside in a candy apple red Porsche full of cash and guns. That would be silly."

Murphy can taste killing this man.

He folds down the liner, drops his steel suitcase into the trunk. Thompson motions to a car across the street. A similar nondescript sedan, but one from this year, starts up then pulls away from the curb. Murphy is pissed at himself for not noticing the car was there.

Needs to be sharper.

He blames this new guy sharing his head.

Mr. Nice Guy better not get me killed.

"Everything we have on Lady Brubaker is on that tablet," Dr. Peyton says. "We'll be monitoring as we always have been. We won't see or hear everything."

"But we'll know enough. Play nice, Murphy." Thompson slams the trunk down, stepping into Murphy's face. "We will not hesitate to pop your top."

"Oooohhh." Murphy fake shudders. "Spooky former Agent Thompson."

"Don't press us on this."

Murphy grins.

He plants a hard kiss on Thompson's lips, holding the sides of his face tight in his hands.

Dr. Peyton grips her tablet tight with her free finger at the ready but has no idea what to do with this. Murphy knows she'll not understand what mix of brain meds to release in this situation. The kiss is long, seems to last a lifetime. Thompson's face flashes red, his eyes popping wide, thrashing side to side fighting to get away. Murphy's grip is strong.

His eyes are closed.

Like you're supposed to.

Murphy releases Thompson's face, letting him stumble backward. Murphy winks, wiping his lips dry. He didn't enjoy the smooch—didn't hate it either—but he loves the fact Thompson and Peyton are constantly on edge with him.

Unpredictability is his only true friend in the world. Needs to keep these people off balance. Always off balance.

"Asshole," Thompson barks.

Murphy snickers.

His laugh starts slow and low but builds. A rolling laughter that goes on and on. Funny at first, but turning to something else. Maniacal in tone.

Hard laughs, almost to the point of choking. Peyton and Thompson look to one another. Murphy can feel a shift inside. Feelings blasting like a shotgun.

Thompson begins to say something, but Peyton stops him.

Murphy's laughter stops as suddenly as it came on. Murphy straightens his back, takes a breath. Bounces on the balls of his feet with his eyes closed. He lets his mind drain clear. His emotions reach out to the corners of himself. Searching for what he needs to know. He knows little about the different parts of him. Nothing human, at least.

"Do I have a home?" Murphy asks.

"Yeah, sure." Thompson shrugs. "Prison is your last known address."

"No. Where am I from?" Murphy continues. "What school did I go to?"

"Murphy. We talked about this." Peyton taps at her tablet. "There's a lot you're simply not going to know. Maybe we can give you more answers later, but you have to remember you're working to reconcile two personalities. Two lives that are very different."

"Do I have any family?" The gears in his mind are shifting hard. "I feel like I do."

"What?" Thompson holds his arms out. "What is all this?"

"Mom, Dad, anything out there? Jesus, tell me there're no kids."

"No children. You have a mother." Dr. Peyton stands between him and Thompson trying to stop what might happen next. "Do you remember her?"

"No." Murphy considers. "Me or the other guy?"

Peyton squints. "Not sure I know who you consider who."

"There's Murphy," Murphy says, "and then there's Mr. Nice Guy."

"Fine," Thompson concedes. "Murphy has a mother. No memories of her?"

"Not at all."

"Good, she's a complete bitch." Thompson's face is still red from the kiss.

"What are you, twelve?" Murphy turns to Peyton. "I want to talk to her."

"Contact with her, that would be..." Dr. Peyton's eyes drift. "That's going to be hard."

"Don't really care about the level of difficulty."

She thinks about it. "Maybe a phone call."

"Maybe?"

Thompson jumps in. "Peyton, absolutely not."

"Wow." Murphy claps his hands loudly. "Really hope Lady Brubaker hasn't burned down a children's hospital since this crap conversation started."

"Murphy, your mother..." Peyton considers. "She's in prison."

Of course she is.

CHAPTER 15

MURPHY WATCHES a house from across the street.

Seems moderately safe, at this distance.

Not sure who is in the house or what he should look for, but he knows this is the place. The house where the now infamous Lady Brubaker was last seen. Murphy has been sitting here ever since the sun went down. It hasn't been long by stakeout standards, but it's been long enough for a mind like Murphy's to begin to wander.

Hard to find comfort when two sets of thoughts roam wild and free.

The massive yard creates a decent amount of space between him and the front door of the upscale home. The dark gives him some cover. But if someone was looking it wouldn't be hard to pick out the eyesore of an automobile Thompson and Peyton gifted him. He toyed with the idea of parking a few blocks from the gated community at an abandoned grocery store then hoofing it to the house, but decided this piece of shit ride would pass as the hired help in this neighborhood.

These decisions are labored.

He used to think much faster.

This added layer. All the comings and goings of judgment and morality have created some speed bumps in Murphy's lightning-like reaction time. Only hopes it doesn't slow him down at the wrong time.

He is thinking more. No question. Analyzing the *shoulds* and *should nots* more than he ever did in the past. Memories have become more like rumors than visions. She said the chemicals inside of him needed to balance. He hasn't had a chance to heal from psychological trauma.

Balance was tricky.

Your mind is a work in progress.

"Jesus," he whispers, wishing he still had that whiskey.

The same lights in the house have been on for quite some time. A possible sign of being left on intentionally. Some small way to keep people from looking at the house as a target. Time-proven tactic by homeowners to ward off the casual break-in. Or something far more sinister.

What if she's in there?

What if Lady Brubaker has taken this house? Muscled control away from the owner to use it as some form of landing spot. A home base of sorts. She has amazing taste if that's the case. If you're going to invade a home, make it a good one.

But is she taking the time to leave the damn lights on?

From what Murphy's seen—and it's not much to be clear—she's not one to give a shit about keeping the neighborhood watch happy. Doubt she'd be the type to set up an old school timer or some kind of AI dimmer system to ward off exactly what Murphy is doing right now. Maybe she's in there with some of her friends from camp. Camp Mind Fucker that the CIA pulled together in conjunction with a forced sponsorship from Dr. Peyton's little company.

He has seen no one come or go.

No movement from the doorways. No shadows moving behind the curtains. No movement of any kind, really. Nothing happening around the garage or any other spot in the house. Has seen no sign of dogs or any pets.

Nothing.

He repeatedly looked over the files from the tablet Peyton gave him. There's not a lot to go on. His eyes ache from pouring over the escape video. Far too many times. Enough times to become even more concerned, even afraid, of what Lady Brubaker and her followers could be up to.

What's even more terrifying to Murphy is the

fact all these people are part of him. Or, more to the point, they have a part of him in them. It is the strangest sensation ever. A new type of relationship. One that has yet to be defined. Not friends. More like brothers and sisters, or shit cousins, but at the same time not even close. He's not sure what to do with it.

New ground he never asked to visit.

He looks over the massive lawn. Thompson and Peyton told him all about who owns this ridiculous, big-money home. An insanely successful hedge fund manager and a close friend to the wealthy. Alec Buckley's fund has a minimum buy-in of over $100 million. A dominant 130-30 fund with superior performance that dwarfs the competition. This puts Buckley in a position to know a lot of people. A lot of insanely powerful, wealthy people.

Is that why Brubaker came here?

Thompson and Dr. Peyton had no idea what she was up to—or so they say. Murphy knows it has to be about money. Almost always is. There are a lot of homes to invade in the world with far less security and risks. No reason to target this individual unless it's about the dollars.

Maybe she's here using his funds, or his access to funds, to build something up. Fund a master plan. Create a war chest of some sort. Or she's using his wealth to transport them somewhere.

Maybe out of the country. Maybe seeking refuge after the CIA attack squads came after them. Find some fast funds and flee the USA for a beach island dream life.

That would make perfect sense.

A shadow flickers upstairs.

The first proof of life he's seen in hours. Instinctively he reaches for his gun. If only for comfort. Fingers wrap around the grip as some kind of odd safety blanket. The volley inside Murphy's mind is difficult to sort. The bounce between terrified and bloodlust. He imagines a life somewhere in the middle. Currently, Murphy has set up shop in the extremes.

A shadow moves from window to window.

His pulse quickens.

The shadow is moving along the upstairs, and then to the lower level. There's a pause. Murphy loses the visual. He blinks, straining to see through the dark. Apparently, it's too much for the almighty agency to throw him some night vision tech.

The shadow appears in the downstairs picture window.

Singular shape.

Can't make out if it's male or female. He or she seems slender. Fit. From the looks of the hedge fund manager's file, he's coming in at 6'4, 300 pounds. This is definitely not that guy in the window. The shadow disappears. No sign of movement. Murphy holds his breath.

The garage door opens.

A red Mercedes four-door backs out of the driveway.

Murphy ducks down into the shadows.

The Mercedes pulls out into the street then speeds up through the neighborhood exceeding the recommended speed limit. He can't see through the driver's blackout-tinted window but there is a driver behind the wheel. He thinks. No way the self-driving AI would break the speed limit. Especially in a residential neighborhood. One other detail catches Murphy's attention. The garage door was left open. Wide open.

A hasty, sloppy exit?

Or inviting me to the slaughter?

Murphy struggles with the very real idea this is a trap. Or perhaps it is simply negligence created by the driver's haste. He entertains the idea of starting up his beaten-to-hell clunker, but realizes he can never catch up to the speeding Mercedes. Also, there's a high probability of being made by the driver.

He looks to his phone then glances to his tablet.

Peyton and Thompson wanted updates. They said he could message them via the phone or tablet with anything that might be helpful. There's more data security on these things than around missile launch codes.

Anything at all, they stressed.

The second they said that, Murphy understood he needed to filter all information internally. He cannot trust either one of them under any circumstances. Murphy decides to table the details of this project for now.

He steps away from the street.

The night air feels good. The blood pumping through his veins feels even better.

"Buckle up," he tells himself.

More like he tells his other half. His less mayhem-friendly Mr. Nice Guy half.

Crossing the street, Murphy checks the homes nearby. There's a lot of space between the residences, by design he's sure. The closest homes are fifty to a hundred yards in every direction. High fences. The wooded area behind his car is deep and backs up to a golf course. There are streetlights but Murphy keeps to the shadows, as if he's doing a dance he's practiced the steps to his entire life.

Alarms, cameras and motion detectors would normally be a massive concern at a house like this one. The place drips of wealth and understandable paranoia. The cameras he won't know about, too small to see and he doesn't have the tech to hunt them down, but the garage door being open is worth a gamble on the alarms.

As he passes from shadow to shadow, he pulls down over his head one of the ski masks that he grabbed from the trunk. The fabric is smooth and soft. A breathable fiber you won't find in the bargain bin. He must check the label for the brand later. These usually come down your face like fresh sandpaper hell.

A memory floods into Murphy's mind.

As real as anything.

He sees himself pulling on a much cheaper ski mask. The scratchiness of the material. It stinks of peanuts and bourbon. All so clear in his mind. As if he wore it yesterday. He feels the mask go over his head and face as he pulls a gun. There's an ocean breeze. The salty taste of the air. The sun shines bright behind him.

He kicks in a door.

Guns blast.

Bodies drop.

An older woman screams at him from the corner.

Murphy snaps out of it. His body trembles. He's seen this memory before. The ski mask is new. That memory was last coupled with his much happier thoughts of the man and woman at the bar. Along with the vision of a rolling car wreck.

Peyton talked about Mr. Nice Guy being killed by a drunk driver.

Is that what he's seeing?

Is the scene at the ocean house one of the many moments that terrified Dr. Peyton? Was this what Thompson was talking about? How he went off the rails and landed on death row in Leavenworth.

He looks to the house.

Is that what's waiting for him in there?

More blood?

As he removes the gun from behind his back, he tests the weight in his hand. It's familiar, and yet it has never been heavier. Mr. Nice Guy has probably never fired a gun before, while the other half has pulled the trigger with as much thought as taking a breath.

He stops. Wait, that's not right.

Mr. Nice Guy knows a little about weapons.

There's a handshake of sorts in his mind.

Was Mr. Nice Guy military too? Not the level of Murphy, but there's a similarity in the way someone trained them in basic. Flashes of those days blur. Drill sergeants scream. Gunshots rattle from the memory of time spent training. Unable to zero in on specifics. Impossible to reconcile.

Mr. Nice Guy was a fit, she said.

His sight slips out of focus. A folding in of thought between the two minds. Murphy wants to sit down and have a drink with his own mind. Wants to keep at it, to push it. Go farther. Dig deeper. There has to be so much more to access. So much more information they're not telling him.

He knows he can't.

Not now.

He looks to the open garage.

Whatever is in that house is the first step. Murphy knows it. Flashes of the lab escape video pop as he closes his eyes tight. The unbridled violence. The soulless rage. The funeral eyes of Lady Brubaker.

She and her friends are out on the loose.

What does she want?

He thinks of the people asleep tonight who don't understand what madness is roaming the countryside. The random violence this homicidal pack is capable of. Something has to be done. Half of him is ready to roll. Half wants to stop and talk about it.

Murphy opens his eyes.

The suppressor attaches. Like holding hands with a long-lost lover.

A warm streak of blood rolls from his left eye.

CHAPTER 16

INSIDE THE HOUSE is exactly what Murphy expected.

A place so nice it pisses you off.

The main lights are off, but the floor dimmers offer a warm glow. Still dark, but the soft fuzz of light along the edge of the darkness is a nice effect. One he couldn't see from the outside, but enough to create a shadow viewable from the outside. Murphy can almost see the bloated price tags on every item in the home.

Fairly sure that was the idea, after all.

These rooms were put together so there was no mistaking the owner's place in the world. The kitchen is steel gray, with pops of black steel. Next-level appliances with the occasional knickknack from a Japanese artist, along with assorted somethings exported from places beyond.

All the lines are clean.

All slicker than shit.

The place stinks of cash, Murphy thinks while holding his Glock, his finger pressing the side of the weapon. Off the trigger for the safety of others.

Murphy hears a low moan echo from the dark.

Sounds like it's coming from down the hall.

Pushing through the doors, across the marble floor of the dining room, he passes a long table for entertaining that could easily seat twenty comfortably.

There are only two places set, however. Thick, tree stump-sized red candles are lit in the center. On either end of the table are plates littered with the scattered remains of what must have been a fine meal. Each plate has a wineglass sitting beside it.

One empty.

One full.

The moan echoes again.

Murphy works through a simple, yet probable, scenario in his mind. Turning it over and over. A little wine, a romantic meal and then some moaning. He can't decide if he wants to walk in on a less than professional sex show or not.

He knows there's another probability as well.

One that involves blood and pain.

Moving toward the sound, Murphy crosses the dining area into a sprawling living room. It is lit with the same soft glow but without the help of candlelight. His scenario has a missing piece, however. Who took off in the Mercedes like a bat out of hell? Staff more than likely wouldn't take off in that car.

Jilted lover?

Is Brubaker a pissed offed date gone wrong?

Moans get louder. He can now tell it's a man.

Murphy steps onto a rug that runs through the living room. Making sure his footsteps make as little noise as possible. Careful to minimize his auditory footprint. More artistic expressions from exotic locations pepper the living area. From behind him, the dining room candles' flames flicker creating dancing shadows along the far wall.

Another, deeper moan.

Is Lady Brubaker screwing him to death?

A small pool of blood lies on the marble a few feet ahead. Smeared and black. Spills and drops lead an uneven path down a hallway. Murphy places his finger on the trigger. The light turns green.

Hate being right all the time.

His senses pull wire tight. Gun raised with both hands, how someone trained him to clear a room. Murphy scans the area with his legs scissoring long strides toward the sound.

His pulse quickens, breathing slows.

He taps the tiny flashlight attached to the barrel of his gun. A two to three-foot area in front of him illuminates. He tilts the gun down every other step to check the dark blood trail below. The moans sound more like cries from here. The mixed prayers for help are hard to mistake.

The trail ends.

Murphy has reached a set of bare feet.

A large, fortysomething male lies naked on the marble floor. A half-dead slab waiting for the drawer. He's bleeding out heavily from his gut with his hands pressing hard to stop the flow. Murphy recognizes him from the files as Buckley the hedge fund god. Above the god—the one bleeding like a pig—is a massive eight-foot oil painting of himself.

Murphy's seen a lot of wounds. Seen a lot of blood.

He knows a dead man when he sees one. At the back of his mind is a person who wants to call an ambulance. *There's a chance we can save him.* He wants to comfort this poor soul no matter how hopeless. That guy—Mr. Nice Guy—is being thrown to the back of the theater. Markus Murphy owns the stage tonight. He has no interest in passing the mic.

"Where is she?" Also not interested in small talk.

"Who are you?" Buckley spits out.

"Look, man." Murphy kneels down. "You've got one, maybe two hours of living left." He's lying; this guy will bleed out in minutes. "I can call someone in and patch your ass up, or I can walk away."

"Please. I have money."

"Don't want your money. What I want is to know where she went. And don't do that *who* bullshit. Neither one of us have the time." Murphy pretends to ponder. "You had a nice meal, thought you were going to get laid, then things went horribly, horribly wrong. Right?" He pets Buckley's head like a pet. "We've all been there. Not me, but I've heard."

"Call someone, you son of a bitch."

"Getting there." Murphy turns. There's a hologram image of a laptop desktop projected, floating in the room next to them. "What was going on in there?"

"I thought she was a pro." Buckley strains to get words out through the pain. "I paid for the girlfriend experience."

"And you got it, brutha." Murphy giggles. "Sorry, keep going."

"She slipped me something in my wine. Forced me to log into my business laptop. I don't know what she's doing. She wanted my clients' information. CRMs, emails."

"Oh yeah?" He moves to the hologram.

He runs his finger up and down scrolling through the screen in midair. Murphy scans through the other open emails.

There are several open with the same subject line—Options for Success.

Murphy takes note. They are all about a meeting taking place in a few days in New York. Fairly nondescript. There are also several open emails to and from one guy.

"Looks like she was digging into a couple of things here. One dude in particular. Zeroed in on a guy named Pruitt. Eryk Pruitt a big deal?"

"Yeah." Buckley would laugh at the question if the hurt wasn't so intense. "He's the CEO of one of the largest tech firms on the planet."

"Ya don't say? Got a lot of folks like this Pruitt in there?"

"I run the largest hedge fund—"

"I know, I get it, you're a really big deal." Murphy stands over Buckley, realizing time is short. He glances above Buckley at the massive painting of him. "That's a horrific picture."

"I can't feel my legs. My fingers."

"Not good." Murphy grips his gun.

Murphy looks to the email projected from the laptop. A floating, three-dimensional rendering of a message that was sent to Buckley from Pruitt telling him how to reach him while he's traveling. Says he's at an exclusive resort.

A resort in Baghdad.

"Okay then." Murphy turns back to Buckley.

"We're almost there. Last question. What's the password."

"Badboyforever99, but without a confirming biometric the laptop will lock up into a brick." Buckley coughs hard. "Come on, man. Fucking help—"

Murphy fires a bullet into his head.

Mr. Nice Guy can only watch on in horror.

Murphy is so glad he used a suppressor.

The gunshot would have echoed through all six thousand square feet of the place.

CHAPTER 17

Shooting Buckley was part mercy, part personal test of will.

Two birds.

Murphy knew Buckley was dead anyway—not long for this earth in any shape or form—and his remaining time would be pure agony. At the same time, he also wanted to see how strong the new dude sharing his head truly was. Needed to know the limits of Mr. Nice Guy. Wanted some confidence in the way this tug of war will play out. The line that cuts between morality conflicts can be uneven in a single mind. Even more so in a group setting.

Is one side stronger than the other?

Is one winning?

Will it always be like this?

As Murphy starts the car, his hands vibrate violently. Barely able to push the ignition. His stomach twists. Pulse pounds. It's as if Mr. Nice Guy has awoken. Perhaps he was napping in an empty corner in his mind.

In a strange way, it's like Murphy is watching another version of himself come undone. Unable to calm him or snuff him out. He pulls the car away from the curb and into the street of Buckley's gated community. His teeth gnash as the emotional flood rolls.

Whispering to himself.

"You did what you had to do."

Numbness setting in.

"This can't be me," escapes his lips.

Doesn't even feel like he said it.

He locks up the brakes. The gate guarding Buckley's community is an inch from his front bumper. Murphy was so adrift in his own head he was seconds away from ramming through the iron. He waits for the luxury community's gate to open. He hacked the cameras into a digital loop before he reached the neighborhood—did that hours ago—but Murphy leaves his mask on all the same. He'll dump the car soon. Knows he needs to make contact with Peyton and Thompson.

The gate slow-swings open.

Murphy presses down the gas slipping out into the night. There's a local bar close. Both parts of him want a drink. At least there's some internal agreement between them.

He needs to reset.

Murphy also knows he needs to put some distance between him and that house, but his need to regroup is becoming nonnegotiable. His entire body shakes. Not going to make it too far in this state of near meltdown.

Feels as if he's physically separating.

Two sides firing shotgun blasts of thought back and forth.

Peyton and Thompson can wait.

Murphy parks the car behind a gas station not far from the house. Stumbling out from the car, his feet barely leave the concrete. Shuffling, dragging, he pulls himself along the side of the car. His hands planted on the steel for support, struggling to make it to the trunk. He pops it open, pulls his things from the back.

Buckley was right about the laptop locking up. Murphy couldn't get more intel from it before the security protocols turned it into a hockey puck, but he took the laptop from the house on the off chance the big brains of the CIA could crack it open.

He did his best to arrange the more interesting emails so he could take a picture with his phone. It's not perfect, but you can make out most of them.

A message popped up on his tablet a few minutes ago letting him know someone would take care of the car. Murphy leaves the laptop covered in the trunk so the government geniuses can do their worst.

Murphy is able to stay inside his head long enough to keep his angles tight. Staying clear of the most likely camera views. Making the dark his friend. The night air helps. Cool and steady. In and out of his lungs like a calming force.

Trying to strong-arm a return to sanity.

A local jazz martini bar is up the road. Murphy saw the joint on the way in. Nice place that's working hard to seem edgy among the wealth of the area. The buffet of exotic cars in the lot destroys any veneer of grit.

He keeps to the side of the road a few feet to the inside of a tree line.

The cool air is nice, but the calming force of whiskey would be better.

He knows he needs to stash his things before going into the bar. Strolling in looking like a half-crazed drifter will not play in a place like this. Checking around his feet, he sees a gathering of leaves and crap from off the trees. He covers his bags in the debris. He'll get them after his drink.

Inside the bar is a small gathering of men and women. Murphy counts five, six if you include the bartender. Bartender seems like he could give Murphy the most trouble. Six feet, give or take, pushing two-fifty, and who the hell knows what he has hidden under the bar.

Slugger?

Shotgun?

Two of the five bar patrons are deep into their sixties. They sit and drink in silence. The other three are in their forties. Wealthy-fit from yoga, hiking vacations and whatever trendy class is working today. Two women and a man laugh with a certain half-in-the-bag sway to them. Multiple dead soldier martini glasses laid to waste in front of them.

Murphy keeps his eyes on the hands and eyes of the bartender. He takes a seat at the corner of the bar. A spot where Murphy can keep everything in front of him and nothing behind him.

The bartender rolls his eyes.

Murphy is forcing him walk to the other side of the bar when all the seats are clearly open. Part of this is because it's the location Murphy wanted to be seated, the other is he wanted to see the bartender move. It will tell him a lot. The bartender is slow. There's a limp brought on by size and weight, or maybe some athletic injury that's been hard on his knees over the years.

This was all in a blink of an eye—the people in the bar, the bartender, and the best location to sit. All processed and assigned a value. Decisions made. Actions taken in seconds. It's not lost on Murphy that he was able to set aside the war inside his head long enough to access the potential points of failure in this bar.

His survival instincts override the conflicts between his dueling personalities.

"What?" the bartender huffs.

Murphy's dark heart glows bright seeing the whiskey is at the other end of the bar. It'll send the bartender back where he just hoofed it over from.

"Whiskey." Said with a bit of *asshole* placed on the word. Resets, then pulls some cash. "Get yourself one too."

Mr. Nice Guy throwing him a bone.

The bartender takes the cash and nods with an eighth of a smile.

"Hope you won," he says before shuffling his big ass to the other side of the bar.

"What's that?"

"Whatever brawl you were in." The bartender points to his eyes. "Hope you got some good shots in."

Murphy looks up, sees his reflection in the mirror just behind the bottles. There are lines of dried blood under both eyes. Muted red splitting the dark bags that hang below his eyes. He shifts to the right slightly behind a bottle to avoid seeing himself.

Toys with the idea of killing the bartender.

He might ID him when the cops come. And they will. The cops will canvas the area asking if they saw anything the night Buckley died. The bartender now has a reason to remember his face.

Murphy shakes off the urge.

Reassures himself that he is somewhat protected by Thompson and Peyton.

He lays down some more cash, picks up his drink and heads to the bathroom. Thankfully, it's a single serve men's room. Locking the door behind him, he turns on the water.

The sound soothes him.

He could use a large dose of soothing right now. He wets his fingers then rubs away the crusted brownish red streaks under his eyes. It flakes and falls into the sink. Mesmerized, he watches it spiral away.

He dries his hands then his face.

One question still eats away—*What does Brubaker want?*

Pulling his phone, he taps one of the only two people the phone can reach.

"Two things. Nonnegotiable." Murphy grips the phone until his knuckles crack.

"I'm listening," Thompson says.

"I want to talk to my mother, and..." Throws back his whiskey. "Get my ass to Baghdad."

CHAPTER 18

THE FOURTEEN-HOUR FLIGHT was far from pleasant.

He was asleep for a goodly portion of the trip. Nestled in the back of the private jet while lost in the embrace of some damn fine sedatives.

Dr. Peyton had them waiting for him at his seat on the flight. She also included a few injections to be administered by the attendant on the flight. Murphy would love to know what the hell is being pushed through his veins, but he knows at this point in the game they've pumped and jammed so much shit into him that questioning the ingredients label is a lost cause.

Calling her an attendant is a bit dismissive. She has a gun, and looks like she'd eat your heart if she chose to. She, Murphy and the pilots are the only people on the plane.

At first, he tried to get some intel from the

heart-eating CIA attendant, but she possesses the personality of a middle finger. Murphy assumes Thompson has a small team in place, and she is part of it. It would need to be small given the nature of all this. More than likely made up of people like the big boy from the hotel, this woman, and perhaps a handful of others. Contract, former military and CIA perhaps. Maybe there are a few researchers left from the grand experiment. Maybe not. Unclear how many died during that nasty escape.

They would need some people to carry out what's going on. There are only a few little bits Murphy could pick up from what Dr. Peyton and Thompson have told him.

They *had eyes on Lady Brubaker* and her friends. The fact they could scramble a private plane to Baghdad off Murphy's single sentence is telling as well.

Trust that you can trust no one.

Someone told Murphy that once.

Wishes he could remember who.

As the plane touches down, Murphy marvels at a country that was once laid almost completely to waste. Now, a city of commerce. A desired destination. A measured mix of Dubai and Cabo. Conferences come here. Businesses outside oil thrive here. People travel here to relax and vacation. He reminds himself you could almost say the same things about Germany, Japan, and Vietnam—to name a few.

War creates travel destinations.

Carnage before cocktails.

Like everywhere he's been since waking up at that shit motel, there's great familiarity here. Much like he felt when he woke up in New York. Somehow, he knows he's traveled the globe, yet doesn't know when and cannot hang on to a single detail. It's possible he's seen the world with no memory of it. A little sad now that he thinks about it.

While he slept during the flight, his standard memories resurfaced.

The bar.

The man and the woman. The happiness. The laughter. The woman playfully bit her lip and fired off a thumbs-up. He also played the darker vision featuring himself. The one of dead bodies in a house on the beach.

This time, as the memory played it was even more vivid. More real. He could smell the gunpowder. There was a ring of gunshots still echoing in the air. His face throbbed as if he took a punch. Hands felt numb from speed loading his weapon. The ocean air blew through the curtains giving a layer of peace over the bloodbath.

This is a memory of Murphy.

The flipping car is still only a flash. A preview of something his mind isn't sharing.

Not yet, at least.

Nothing like the scene from the bar where he's watching. Removed from happiness but still a witness to it. No, the beach house is a recollection of something horrible where he was the main attraction, rather than a member of the audience.

What did you do?

I did what had to be done.

You've killed a lot people, haven't you?

Wow, you're a perceptive pussy aren't you.

It's worse than that—you enjoy killing people.

"Shut your little bitch mouth," Murphy says.

The heart-eating woman raises her eyebrows, lowers her book.

"Not you." Murphy turns back to staring out the window.

As he sits feeling the warmth of the sun across his face, he can't believe he's become that crazy person with voices arguing morality inside his head.

That shit needs to stop.

He's now a various-minded man. Oh, to be single-minded.

"Any whiskey on this bucket?" Murphy asks.

"Put a bottle in your bag." She returns to her book. "For what it's worth, I hope you kill her."

"What's that?"

"That woman—Brubaker—hope you kill her."

Murphy nods, considers asking for more, but

doesn't. He assumes Lady Brubaker and her friends are responsible for the deaths of a few friends of Agent Heart Eater.

Makes Mr. Nice Guy feels slightly better about this trip. Not much, but marginally. A thin veneer of nobility via murder helps a bit. It's a slippery slope, Murphy knows, but if Mr. Nice Guy finds comfort in the "killing for a cause angle" then maybe this can work.

The plane slows to a stop.

"Oh yeah." She hands Murphy a phone with a small scrap of paper taped to the back. "Call your damn mother."

CHAPTER 19

Murphy moves through the lobby of the resort.

Taking it all in while continuously scanning for two people.

Eryk Pruitt and Lady Brubaker.

He can't, however, shove aside how impressive the lobby truly is. Best he can tell it stretches the length of several football fields. A giant fish tank rests in the center with two large sharks circling the blue as if watching over the lobby. There's a waterfall gently falling in the distance, with several restaurants in view. The place is buzzing with families rushing to the pool. Young-money-sexy-people from around the world casually glide across the marble as if they own the place. Even the air seems like it was handcrafted by a team of experts.

On the way from the airport, the driver told Murphy that Baghdad has made a concerted effort to step up its hotel and resort game in recent years.

Tired of losing money to Dubai, Singapore and the like. A perfect place for a single, master of the universe, technology CEO to hang out and recharge with a homicidal prostitute.

No less than three kindly people have asked to help with his bags, but Murphy felt it best to carry his own shit. There are some very strict laws in this country. Some still carry consequences that involve limbs being removed. All of his firearms have been carefully stowed on the plane back at Baghdad International with Agent Heart Eater.

He's also not excited by the prospect of some hotel employee discovering his bag of doctor-prescribed knock-out-a-psycho injectors and other bids and bods he's got on him.

He can't think of the last time he didn't have a gun.

Then again, he still doesn't remember much before a few days ago.

No, ladies and gentlemen, for the duration of his stay Markus Murphy will be armed with a knife, cash, military-grade sedatives and unrelenting charm. Part of him is arrogant enough to think that's enough. Part of him wants to get to his room as quickly as possible, pull the curtains and order room service.

Given Pruitt's status and wealth, Murphy is guessing he should be easy to track. Look for multiple well-dressed employees and where they flock to. Seek out the high-end services areas of the grounds. He'll ask the front desk about their luxury packages.

Then, he'll ask what's above that.

He'll take a quick tour and ask if they have dedicated staff for the VIPs. Ask about what's available at the pool for people cut from a better cloth. Private dining options? Keep probing until he finds where they hide the upper crust from the commoners.

Murphy enters the mirrored elevator.

He holds himself perfectly still, then looks up letting the elevator scan his eyes. The top floors require special access.

Murphy got a sweet penthouse suite.

He decided he needed something special so he, ya know, could be in the same general area where Pruitt and Brubaker might be located. Since someone else is picking up the tab, what the hell? It also helps with getting information. Helps with the narrative he's one of the *them*. Part of the money crowd. At least that's the story he's pitching to management and whoever else requires a dose of bullshit.

Murphy doesn't remember much about himself, but there's this strong sense that money wasn't part of his upbringing. Neither side of him. There's an odd tension; he's not completely comfortable with all this luxury. Feels undeserved.

Unnecessary. Maybe one side of him lived well in recent years—death and chaos does pay well—but Murphy and Mr. Nice Guy were both raised shitty.

No doubt on that one.

So, he grabs a champagne glass off a passing tray.

Murphy doesn't know how far ahead of him Lady Brubaker is right now. Pruitt may already be dead for all he knows. But the quick math dictates that she only has about an hour jump on him, at best. Not like she could drive that sweet-ass, stolen Mercedes here. She can't speed up how long it takes to get to Baghdad from NYC, and he's guessing, she doesn't have access to a private plane.

But she might.

Everything is a big fat question mark right now.

The dead hedge fund douche said he thought she was a high-end prostitute. Stands to reason that's her angle. From what he's seen she's attractive, smart, manipulative. Wealthy, unattractive men have a hard time not paying up for that menu.

She'll more than likely use that as her ticket with Pruitt. Maybe that's how she'll make the introduction. Open a conversation with the common connection they share with the hedge fund douche.

She'll leave out that she cut him open, of course.

Never let the truth fuck up a good story.

Murphy lets his bags bounce on the bed. He'd like nothing more than to crawl in between the crisp sheets and nap-out for a few days. That much both sides of him can agree with. The room service menu on the table by the bed is calling his name. Bet there are some good movies he could watch. The room is immaculate. The temperature is perfect.

Dammit.

The sprawling hotel suite is stark white with slight hints of chrome, perhaps platinum, peppered here and there. There's a long dresser made from polished concrete and two red leather chairs between the window and the door.

The room looks lab clean. Plush. Expensive. A living magazine. Looks like a picture from someone you hate who's living better than you.

Murphy pulls out the phone he got when the plane landed.

The handwritten note stuck to the back simply reads:

Your mother will call from prison in 3 hours and 26 minutes.

CHAPTER 20

DOESN'T LEAVE much time for Brubaker hunting.

It took about an hour to get to the hotel from the airport.

Murphy does not know why Mr. Nice Guy wants to talk to this woman. This mother. Mr. Nice Guy screams out from the cheap seats. He's worming his way into Murphy. Mr. Nice Guy wants to connect with family.

Of course he does.

Sad sack.

That guy wants to chat with her, but Murphy isn't interested in that clown's need for answers. The need for emotional closure or whatever-the-hell is not something Murphy yearns for.

It is Murphy's mother for fuck's sake, and Murphy isn't interested in connection.

The two sides of him seem to have become more divided since he left New York. Seemed for a moment like the two made some progress, but perhaps not. Is this the tricky balance Dr. Peyton talked about? Or is this how it is supposed to be. Two warring factions in his mind working against one another to find the best, most stable middle ground.

Sounds about right.

One of them wants to hunt and kill.

The other wants to run to Mommy.

Again, the mommy in question is actually the mother of the one who wants to hunt and kill.

The ins and outs are exhausting.

Murphy's mother—like everything else in his mind—floats without weight. Untethered. He holds no clear recollection of her. Only a feeling toward her, and it is not a positive one.

Maybe he left things badly last time they saw one another. Certainly possible—anything is possible right now—but if a brief conversation with her will soothe Mr. Nice Guy's bullshit and allow them to take care of the task at hand, then so be it.

"Lovely, isn't it?" the man asks.

Murphy snaps out of his trance.

The nice, thin man with the most delicate of features at the front desk has been very helpful. Murphy barely remembers chatting him up after leaving his room.

The delicate man from the front desk is showing Murphy the massive infinity pool that seems to bleed into the Tigris River even though the river is miles away. An optical illusion that works well. A peaceful oasis to kill for. The temperature is cool, for around here, but still warm enough to hang out by the pool.

"The private cabanas are located over there." The tiny man points to a line of what amounts to high-end tents guarded by palms. "And beyond that wall is the exclusive pool for our special guests."

"Oh yeah, how special?"

"Very special, sir."

"May I see?"

"Perhaps your next visit. We can make the reservation today if you like."

"What about dining options? Spots for a cocktail?" Murphy notes the time on his phone. The sun will go down soon. Better odds of finding Pruitt and/or Brubaker at dinner or drinks.

"Oh, we have some magnificent options for you to choose from."

"No, where do those *special* people graze? The ones at the pool beyond the wall."

"Mr. Howard." Murphy almost forgot that he checked in under the name *Howard*. The thin, delicate man parses his lips. "Those are considered some of the finest dining establishments in the world. They are booked months, in some cases, a year in advance and—"

"Really? No way to find a seat on short notice?" Murphy produces a roll of Iraqi dinar for the thin, delicate man to see. A solid half an inch of currency.

"Table for one." Murphy looks him over. "Find a place for a special bitch like Mr. Howard?"

"Of course, Mr. Howard." The thin, delicate man snatches the wad with a smile as wide as the sun. "I'll send someone to escort you."

"No need, my man," Murphy says. "Tell me where to go, what time, and point me to a bar that's not too far."

CHAPTER 21

THE JOINT IS slick if nothing else.

Open-air dining with candles that hover above the center of white tablecloth tables. First time Murphy has seen tiny drones used for candleholders, but it is pretty cool. The sun is still out but fading fast. Just enough darkness to keep the temperature cool and the atmosphere even cooler. Everything is in its right place. Various forks and spoons located properly. Wine and water glasses positioned to catch the flickers of the flames that hover slightly above them.

Wasn't easy to find this place.

It amazes Murphy how they can hide an entire restaurant, but they did. Nothing signals that this place is here or how to get here. The thin, delicate man from the hotel gave him directions while checking over his shoulder every couple of seconds. Murphy felt he was putting on a bit of a show.

No way in hell he's never taken a taste to let someone in this place.

Murphy stopped by a shop that caught his eye on the way into the hotel. A high-end men's clothing store with some fine threads showcased in the window. He thought he needed to get dolled up for the evening. Look the part. The thin, delicate man also mentioned there was an event of sorts going on this evening. Actually, it was something the resort puts on from time to time. Special menu with extra sexy staff and the resort overpays the hell out of a global music sensation to come play a set or two while the elite stuff their faces.

Murphy loves the hell out of a good suit.

Gray pinstripes, white shirt, pink tie and black shoes that shine like mirrors. He also has a tactical blade secured behind his back. Really misses his Glock right now.

Longs for the green lights lit up from firearm recognition. Fear is absent, at the moment, but Murphy has seen a brief preview of what Brubaker is capable of and would rather not walk into a potential showdown without a gun.

Oh well.

The crowd is thin but growing.

Global elite, and Murphy, gathering under the stars. Murphy has taken a seat at the corner of the bar near the entrance. Perfect vantage point for overlooking the tables and the people coming and going. Sipping his whiskey, scanning the area, he begins to question his plan. Gnawing questions he'd rather not consider.

What if Pruitt has other plans this evening?

What if Brubaker has already killed him and fled the country?

He tells himself again the timing on her bouncing out of Baghdad would be a challenge. But still not impossible. Has to trust his gut with this. There was no way the resort would give up Pruitt's room number, and hacking the system wasn't realistic given the time constraints and the high risk of an international incident if discovered. Yes, this is the best option he's got for a hunting ground.

Mr. Nice Guy is nervous.

Murphy tells him to let the other nut drop and shut the hell up.

Another sip of whiskey.

He checks his phone. Not long until this scheduled call with his mother is going down. Murphy has no idea what to expect from the conversation. Only knows that at least a part of him doesn't want to have it.

Thompson didn't want him to talk to her either—*why?*

Questions stack, climbing over the top of one another.

Doubt creeps in. An unwanted gift from Mr.

Nice Guy, Murphy assumes. Doubt is for other people. *Those people.* Not for Markus Murphy. Crazy fills in the holes doubt creates.

Murphy drinks to that.

Drinks to crazy over doubt.

"Right this way, Mr. Pruitt."

Murphy fights the urge to spin around. As he casually turns, he sees Eryk Pruitt move across the turf-like grass being led toward a table for two. One of the best—if not the best table—in the place. Close to the stage, but far enough to enjoy the evening. He's alone, dressed in a casual suit that looks past its prime. Cheap looking by design, but far from it. Curated, high-priced retro.

He's in his late thirties with a shaved head, glasses and appears to be in good shape. Doesn't seem the type who has to pay for top-dollar entertainment, but Murphy isn't one to judge. He seems to favor his right side. Murphy takes note. He doesn't expect getting into a physical altercation with Pruitt, but again, anything is possible and knowing he's right-handed might be helpful. Pruitt takes his seat with the hovering candlelight creating a glow to his face.

Murphy gets up from his seat at the bar.

Might not get another, or a better, chance to talk to Pruitt. A chance to find out what he knows about the hedge fund house. About a prostitute who might desire causing him great harm.

Pruitt turns toward the bar. His eyes dead on Murphy.

Murphy stops, holds his breath. *Has he made me?*

"Whiskey," a woman's voice says.

Murphy turns.

A woman with dark hair with the tips colored purple takes a seat a few chairs down from him. Colorful tats cover her arms. Flowers and thorns mixed with interesting shapes and the large face of a gray wolf on her shoulder. She wears a black dress like a weapon. Gorgeous, terrifying, and the someone who could possibly save or end Murphy's life. He can't help but stare—for multiple reasons.

He exhales, fighting to find cool.

She locks in on his eyes. Her expression like a stone. A hard and angry stare lasting longer than Murphy would like. His brain scrambles for ways to break the wire-tight tension. A violent awkwardness. Her death stare matches what he saw in the video. Before he can get out a single word, her hardness softens without warning. Eyes show a flash of light as her expression melts into a smile.

"Enjoying the view?" she asks with some sass. "Not free."

Murphy raises his glass. He didn't run this as a probable scenario.

"Penthouse five, Royal level." He smiles.

Burning on pure instinct. "The suit is new so, ya know, use the gentle cycle."

"Get in line, Big Fun." Lady Brubaker snickers, slipping away with her drink.

Pruitt stands from his table as she walks in his direction. Part of Murphy thinks he should warn him. Thinks he should stop her. Prevent whatever horrific act she's planning with that poor, insanely wealthy bastard.

"Not the sort to wait in line, gorgeous," Murphy says.

She stops, turning his way. "You don't say."

"A lot of pretty ladies around here." He taps a money wad that could choke an elephant. "I mean look at me. This suit. This face. This cash. *Lonely* is not in my future."

She considers.

"Going once..." He strokes the cash.

She eyes the money.

"See you soon," she says with syrup. "Might get dirty on that Royal level."

Murphy tips his glass to her as she walks away. His heart pounds while his fumbling insides fight to be cool. Both sides of him buzz with a mix of excitement and terror.

Pruitt pulls out a chair for her.

She lets out a schoolgirl giggle, throwing him a soul-melting smile as she slides into her chair. Murphy searches deep. Working to uncover some mental middle ground within himself. He should stop her. Working through the moral math, he resets.

Pruitt is a dead man.

Lady Brubaker is Murphy's target.

A target, that if handled properly, could save many, many other lives including his own. Murphy downs his drink, celebrating the emotional growth achieved.

His jacket vibrates. Murphy pulls out the phone.

Mother is calling.

Shit.

CHAPTER 22

Murphy said "Hello" to his mother ten minutes ago.

Feels like hours have limped by.

Since this call began, she's coughed twice, grunted once.

He can tell she's still on the line because the sounds of prison-crazy ramble and rage in the background. Some woman offered a full-throated wail about cutting another woman's tits off. There have been various random shouts echoing similar thoughts and sentiments. Another sign that the call is still in progress is the sound of her labored breathing. The sounds of a lifelong smoker stress the phone's speaker. Murphy closes his eyes off the wheezing.

A loud clang from her end of the call shakes him from his trance. More bodily harm threat barked, then more struggling breaths. Murphy doesn't know how much more of it he has to endure.

This is a game she's playing.

He knows it.

The game of control.

Give her time, Mr. Nice Guy chimes in.

Entering the lobby of the resort en route to the elevator, Murphy still waits for her to speak her first words. She doesn't have to speak until she wants to; he knows that too. He can't make her talk. The thing, the only thing, working in his favor is that there's no way in hell she has unlimited phone privileges. She has to crack open a can of conversation soon.

It's also a fair assumption that every word of this call is being monitored, recorded and analyzed to the nth damn degree.

You happy, Mr. Nice Guy?

This the quality family time you seek?

His devil tattoo itches. Warmth spreads up through his arm. A reversal in Murphy's thinking takes hold. A switch flipped. Peyton is working her magic. She knew when this call was happening too.

Does she want more Mr. Nice Guy than Murphy?

Fifty percent Murphy the proper mix?

He imagines Dr. Peyton sitting sipping a hot cup of tea, balancing his brain as if pulling together a grocery list. Something inside of him takes over. Finding words becomes easier. Wanting to say words to his mother becomes easier. He envisions Peyton sliding her fingers along the glass. Altering his chemistry as he speaks.

"You don't have to talk if you don't want to, Barbara." A warm tone he didn't realize he had to offer. He didn't know her name seconds ago, but it fell from his tongue as if he talked to her yesterday. "I only wanted to reach out. Let you know I'm thinking of you."

"You are a piece of shit." Her voice is raspy, thick with a southern drawl.

"Pardon?"

"How goddamn dare you."

"Okay. Not sure what you're—"

"I'm locked up in this piss-pit because of you. And now you're doing what? Out there nailing strange ass and killing at will?" She hacks up a lung. "This what you want, Mr. Fancy Balls? Call me up? Tell Mommy all about it? Have ourselves super sweet bullshit convo, you deviant little asshole."

Murphy—Mr. Nice Guy—takes a beat. Hopes that wave has ended.

"Locked up because of me?" He braces for the answer. Wanting to know more.

"Oh, stop that shit."

"Just need—"

"Please cease with whatever game you're playing."

"No, please. No game. I don't have time to explain it all, but I don't remember." Murphy enters the elevator, letting it scan his eyes for identification. "Why are you there? Is it because of something I did to you?"

"You've got some set of grapes don't you, boy? Didn't get those from your daddy, that's for goddamn sure. That pansy-ass had a sack of toddler nuts."

"Barbara—"

"And what's with all this *Barbara* bullshit? I'm your mother for fuck's sake."

"Sorry... Mom. What happened?"

There's a long pause.

"Mother." Hacks again. A prison scream in the background. "You call me Mother. That's the thing. Always has been."

"Okay." Murphy sucks in a deep breath through clinched teeth. "Mother. Please tell me what happened."

"You best not be dicking me around with this not remembering shit."

"I'm not. Please talk to me."

"Better be playing it straight, boy."

"I am." An uncontrollable surge inside of Murphy rips. Blows past Mr. Nice Guy like he was standing still. "Talk to me, you whacko fucking whacko."

Another stretched pause.

Deep sigh from someone who has nothing to lose.

"Fine. Don't yell at me," she says. "I needed some help, that's all. Was having a little money problem, just like everybody does from time to time, and I brought you a job. A simple little bang-bang thing. Should have been nothing for a badass like yourself. It tilted a wee bit sideways, and you went fifty shades of apeshit."

The elevator beeps.

The doors opened a while ago. Murphy doesn't remember holding them open.

Heading down the hall, he walks toward penthouse number five pressing the phone tighter to his ear. As if trying to push it into his brain to gain a better understanding.

"You got that look you get sometimes. All in your eyes," she continues. "You snapped, like you did as a child. Got all kinds of dicked up."

"What was the job?" he asks as the door scans him in.

"This don't make any kind of goddamn sense, boy. You call me out of the blue, haven't talked to you since God knows when, and now you're asking dumbass questions about that?"

"Barbara... Mom..."

"No, no. This ain't right. Can smell your bull-shit from here."

"Please, Mother. Don't shut down on me."

More silence.

A cough, then the call goes quiet. Nothing but dead prison air on the other end of the phone. Murphy paces back and forth in the hotel suite. He can still hear the sounds of her world in the back-ground. Can still hear the hard work it takes for her to breathe. He fights the urge to press her. To pull a conversation out of her. The desire to scream at her is unbearable, almost too much to hold back. The rage swells. Brand of rage that only comes from childhood. Mr. Nice Guy knows all about child-hoods that break you.

He wants a turn. Mr. Nice Guy wants another try at her.

"Mother?"

She says nothing. The grinding quiet continues.

Murphy grabs the bottle of whiskey Agent Heart Eater packed for him then heads into the bathroom. He's lost track of the time and his poten-tial *date* with Lady Brubaker could be any minute.

Mr. Nice Guy needs to go away.

He needs to leave and come back some other day. Murphy's arriving guest does not seem like the patient sort. Unfortunately, Mr. Nice Guy is still here. Taking center stage in his mind and deeply wanting to connect with Murphy's dear, sweet mother.

Seek to understand.

"We can talk about anything. Tell me how you are. Talk to me about anything you want. I'm a blank slate here. I want to reset. Start over. Can we try that?" He considers his words. "I'm sorry. Sorry for what I did."

Nothing.

Mr. Nice Guy feels horrible for something he had nothing to do with, while Murphy is considering blowing both his brains out. Murphy is drained. Exhausted. He can tell another shift is on the way. His chemistry is changing.

The silence drags for days.

She coughs. She grunts.

"When in the hell did you become such a pussy?" she asks.

"Okay. Fine, Barbara." He swallows back the urge to remove her head.

"If you can't muster the word *Mother*, so help me."

"Sorry, *Mother*. Need some time calling you that, okay?" Grips the phone, knuckles popping.

"Not too much to ask, is it?"

"No. Got it." He rubs his face. Shuts his eyes in self-defense. Murphy takes back control. "Look, Mother, I've got to go. Have a meeting, but we'll talk again soon."

"Soon?" She cough-chirps. "Soon—"

Tapping a merciful end to the call, he sets his phone down on a towel. Glancing to the mirror, he studies himself. Sees how tired he truly is. Resembles a match that's been snuffed out.

Calls with Mother are like that.

Murphy rubs his neck where his head and spine collide. The war in his skull wages on. A conflict that started in New York and has no foreseeable end to the hostilities. One he didn't start. He's also finding a real feel for the pain and the various levels it offers.

Dead might be better.

Murphy bounces this idea off the walls of his mind. Probably best he doesn't have a gun right now.

Dead could be better than this.

This. This is like the worst hangover after the best night. Murphy would, however, prefer the sloppy joy that comes along with this feeling. This rumble in his brain is happening more and more. Happening with more unsolicited intensity.

They said it would get better.

They said a lot of shit.

CHAPTER 23

MURPHY SWIPES his fingers in the air, turning on the sink.

Water falls like focused rain from an unseen spout under the mirror. He lets it run, wants to get the water nice and cool. The sound is soothing. A large dose of soothing is needed right now.

A dull pain in his head mounts.

He fills a glass, chugs it, then fills it again before swiping off the water. The bathroom is so quiet it hums.

The pain amplifies.

Grinding his teeth, he spreads his fingers out on the bathroom counter. Palms flat, the webbing of his fingers stretched wide. His fingertips and palms feel the smooth stone mixed with tiny, rough imperfections. Hopes the coolness of the hotel's polished concrete will offer some comfort.

It does not.

Murphy braces for what's coming.

Thoughts of Mother fade.

Brubaker is coming his way.

His eyes stare out like barrels of a shotgun. Breathing in and out, Murphy tries to focus on that elusive happy spot inside his ravaged mind. Something he's only been able to see during fleeting moments of unconsciousness. He sucks in deep, lungs filling, while his splintered brain hunts for that sneaky chunk of calm.

There's that memory he's become rather fond of.

A comfy little mind-spot. A moment of bacon-wrapped peace. He can only hope it's real.

Even now, he's not sure it's an actual memory.

His fingers press harder, as if trying to stab through the concrete counter to gain a grip. To hold on to his eye of the storm. Jaw clenches. Eyes close tight. He's found it.

His maybe-memory

It pours over him like a synaptic downpour of sweet syrup. He holds his breath. His heart skips a row of beats. The memory is slipping. The fingertips of his mind claw at it only to watch it fumble and slip off into the void.

"Shit."

Eyes open, hard breaths now push between clenched teeth.

Murphy waits for the inevitable to materialize in the mirror.

Blood rolls down from his eyes.

First the left, then the right. Dual deep-red ribbons run down his cheeks. Tiny drops drip, littering the counter and sink. Staring back at him in the mirror is a familiar yet still oddly unfamiliar man.

He snickers. Snort-laughs while his body shakes.

Blood tears slide around his nostrils before slipping over his curled lip. He whips his tongue across his lips with a lizard-like swipe. Upper, then lower, wiping them into a smeared form of clean. Murphy dumps the water from his glass into the sink, then grabs the bottle of whiskey. He twists it open with his teeth, spitting the cap out into the empty bathtub.

Smiles big and broad.

Doesn't know the mix, but it's high on the Murphy side.

The thick edge of the hotel glass clinks against the mouth of the whiskey bottle. Murphy's shaking hands fight for a proper long pour. Booze splatters and splashes on the counter and floor. Murphy sucks some spill from the back of his hand, taking pride in the fact he got most of it into the glass. Like a young boy who hit the toilet, mostly.

He adjusts his pink tie.

Fixes his starched white collar so it lies correctly over the jacket of his gray pinstriped suit.

There's a knock.

Murphy stops. *A whole lot of violence is at my door.*

His breathing evens. Slows. Heartbeat works a steady beat. The blood streams gain momentum. He wipes under his eyes with the back of his hand. Not wanting this pesky issue to ruin the overall look he has going.

Might not get another shot at Brubaker.

He inspects his work in the mirror. A brownish red smear is spread across his face, looking like a nasty clown who was slapped silly. He winces as he wets a towel with some whiskey from the bottle for better cleanup.

Another knock.

Another snort of whiskey. Holds his hands out straight. The shaking has slowed but still there. Mr. Nice Guy mutters something at the back of his mind.

Murphy slaps his face.

Waits, then slaps himself again, only harder.

Murphy adjusts his tie.

Shrugs, takes a jerk straight from the whiskey bottle before spinning himself into the living room of the sprawling hotel suite. The massive television shows his now favorite hotheaded news program. Brightly colored graphics frame a well-dressed, handsome man passionately pounding a desk about the crisis that led to violent riots the media has so casually named the *Cash Clash.* Or the more callous *Snobs versus Slobs.*

"The current financial crisis makes the Great Depression look like heavy petting." The British man's face glows redder and redder with each word. Others around him nod their heads in faithful agreement.

Murphy swats at the wall-screen as if shoeing a fly.

The wall goes mute. He adjusts the two red leather chairs—the few items in the room not blinding white—so the chairs are facing one another. Getting the angles right where he wants them.

Murphy tells the curtains to open.

They split, spreading to reveal the final moments of a stunning sunset over Baghdad. The suite's eye-candy view overlooks the enormous infinity pool complete with rushing waterfalls on either side. In the distance, hints of the lowering sun bounce off the Tigris River like a retreating fireball who's finished today's shift.

Thoughts of the escape video flood his mind.

Part of him loves the art of it. Part of him does not.

The knock at the door is harder, angrier this time.

"Hold please," he singsongs at the door.

Murphy fishes around his grab-bag mind, finding the fakest smile in the history of fake smiles. He throws open the door.

Lady Brubaker stands in the hallway.

"Hi," Murphy almost sings.

He's struck again by how she wears that dress. A weaponized woman with green eyes that carve through the world.

They cut through Murphy, he can't lie.

She smiles at him like there's no place she'd rather be. He can safely assume her true smile has long since disappeared. She pushes past Murphy like an unnecessary turnstile, taking a stance in the middle of the room. Wants Murphy to make a meal of the view.

"Come on in." Not giving her the satisfaction.

Murphy shuts the door. Locks it. He smiles again. The woman puts on a nice smile, but deep down he knows she could not be any more disinterested.

This is business.

Ugly business.

Mr. Nice Guy's services are not needed here.

Perhaps she's going through some similar issues, he thinks.

"We gonna do this?" Unzips her dress as if she's taking out the trash.

"Hey, whoa. Easy." Holds up his hand. "Let's

talk. Get to know you style chitty-chat." Offers her the red chair by the window. He wants the one by the door. He'd prefer to block the exit if at all possible. "Please. Drink?"

Brubaker drops her fake smile, rolling her eyes as she slides down into the chair by the door. Murphy takes the unwanted seat across from her, accepting his minor defeat. She unwraps a cherry lollipop, plopping it on her tongue. Rolling it, sucking it between her deep purple coated lips. Annoyed, but always pushing the sexy.

A pop, a crack, then a boom sounds off from outside the window. The fireworks display is cranking up. Flashes of exploding color ripple across the room. Neither one of them jump or show a hint of anxiety. The booms echo as the room fades into a quiet, still state.

This moment of silence is deafening.

Eyes fire bullets.

"Well." Murphy claps his hands. "Okay, now—"

"Stop." Slips the lolly from her lips. "What is all this?"

"What's what?"

"The bar. At the bar, we already talked. You liked what you saw. You asked me to come here. Sooo..." She jams the lolly back into her cheek. "Start your engines, Big Fun. Or my sweet ass walks."

"Yeah, you don't have to pretend, *Sweet Ass*. Playtime is wrapping up." Holds up a finger. "Now, don't get me wrong. You're gorgeous. No argument. But sticky sexy time ain't what's on my mind... Lady Brubaker."

Her eyes flare.

She sucks the lolly harder, as if the center holds some answers.

A bonfire dances behind those green eyes. Brings a dirty smile to her face. A genuine one. She nods her head, studying him harder now.

"Your eyes." She leans in with a knowing smirk. Motions to the remains of his blood tears. "They, well, honestly, they don't look great."

Murphy shrugs, noticing a tiny flake of red clinging just below her nostril. Some papers in the files said some of them might bleed from their noses.

"Sucks." Lady Brubaker gives an understanding nod. "Doesn't it?"

"It does. It really does."

"Headaches?"

"Hmmm, hate those."

Faster than a blink, Brubaker pulls a knife from the inside of her thigh. Perhaps a blade from Japan, Murphy notes. She sits up straight like a cobra. Eyes wild and wide. Murphy is struck by her glee. They usually reserve this level of joy for parents of a fresh newborn. The blade of her knife is shiny-wet, slick with smears of blood.

"It's a damn shame, right?" Holds her knife like an impatient surgeon. "They make it sooo hard to get guns into this country."

Murphy whispers a soft, "Yes."

He snaps his fingers as if remembering something.

Murphy pulls his Ka-Bar combat blade from behind his back. Cold. Clean. Black military-grade steel. Resting the knife on his thigh, he ever so slightly digs his designer shoes into the carpet. Ready to launch himself forward if necessary. He thinks of the super-needles Peyton and Thompson gave him. Resting in the suitcase near the bed. He wants to jam the Ka-Bar into his thigh for being the type of idiot that would leave them over there.

Lady Brubaker grips her messy, Japanese blood-blade.

Fireworks pop then boom outside. Exploding sparkles light up the night, blanketing the room in flickering shards of light. A fresh spark of silence.

Lady Brubaker pops her lolly out from her lips then flings it behind her.

"Your knife there..." Murphy makes a yuck-face at the blood. "Kinda gross."

"Right?" Tilts her head birdlike. "Yours looks a little neglected. You know what to do with that thing?"

Lady Brubaker's gaze is like a funeral.

Murphy's smile is cold.

"Part of me does," he says.

"I'm sure it does." Her eyebrows dance. "Markus Murphy."

CHAPTER 24

Murphy's blood runs cold.

"Oh yeah, I know you." Lady Brubaker's eyes flare, reading his zeroed-out expression. "I know Dr. Peyton. Only by name, unfortunately. Love to meet her. Thompson—that guy I know all too well. But you? You're my super, special favorite boy."

"You knew I'd come here."

She nods.

"You made it easy." Searches his thoughts while speaking. "Made it simple to find you."

"Shhh." She presses two fingers to his lips, casually flipping her hair back.

Murphy's thoughts burn.

Feelings race to the surface, burst, then turn to dust. He's peeling away again. Tiny pieces of him drifting off the bone like burning paper flaking and floating. Unable to shake his focus from the blood that shines along the blade of her knife.

He thinks of the injectors, useless in his suitcase near the bed.

"The stability of things has been teetering for generations." She thumbs toward the news show as they continue debating the Cash Clash. "The delicate balance between the penthouse and the shithouse. A thin hair holding it back from the fall. We didn't start it..." She stands up from her chair, looking down at him. "But we're pleased as punch to push it over the edge."

Murphy rises to his feet, gripping his knife tight in his fist.

She steps closer.

"*They* probably told you all kinds of things, right? Bet *they* failed to mention one fun fact, however. The fact I can shut it down. I can stop the party we have planned." She snaps her fingers. "Just like that. All they have to do is give me what I want."

"And that is?"

"We'll get there." Eyes wild and wide, locked into his. "Our way. Nobody can stop us. Okay?"

Murphy stops. There's something familiar in what she just said.

The words she's chosen.

He's heard them before.

"What did you say?"

"You know what? Think I'll take that drink now. But..." Lady Brubaker considers, running her tongue over her teeth. "Don't dare drink yours first."

Murphy's mind scratches, claws to remember.

His eyes drift. Shoulders inch up.

Then...

She bites her lower lip, then gives him a thumbs-up.

Everything stops.

Murphy's mouth goes dry. Words catch, held captive in his throat.

The man and the woman at the bar. His favorite memory that's buried so deep. Brubaker mirrored the scene from his broken mind. Identical to what he's seen played over and over.

Murphy's once shotgun stare now floats like a freighted child's.

How does she know that?

Does she have the same memory as Murphy?

No.

Something is different.

A flicker of that favorite memory pops among his fumbling thoughts. Only for a splinter of a moment, but he sees the scene from a new point of view. That woman at the bar. Her beautiful face in front of him. Standing in front of Murphy as if he was the bartender.

"Tell me something. This thing they turned you into. This... *Murphy*?" Scrunches her nose. "Is he just like you? Is he a playground wrapped in barbed wire?"

A word forms inside his mind.

A name screaming out in the middle of a riot.

A name he can't put a face to. One that's not connected to a person, but a name that is becoming clearer and clearer. Then, soft like a gentle cry, that name slips from his lips.

"Kate?"

Lady Brubaker plunges her knife into his stomach.

Murphy's body jerks.

Face falls.

He struggles to ask *why?*

She kisses him, robbing the question from his open mouth. Running her fingers over the side of his trembling face, she turns him. Steering him with the knife as blood spills over her hand. She shoves him free from her blade, down into the chair he so carefully moved in front of the door.

"You can have that chair now." She taps him on the nose.

Murphy sits helplessly, holding his wound.

Eyes open. Lost.

Fireworks boom.

Lady Brubaker walks out the door without looking back.

CHAPTER 25

KATE.

The name echoes.

Soft, restrained, then loud and clear.

Like a name close to him. A name he's said over and over but still can't place where or when. Knowing that he is known as somebody else is the strangest of sensations, but not being able to place the people and events within his own head stretches the boundaries of bizarre.

His thoughts ignite. A synaptic brushfire.

Memories animate to life forming with color and light. Sights and smells. Only to have those memories break off into clumsy chunks bouncing away from him. Each one fighting to maintain its life in his mind only to crumble into rubble.

Murphy can see it all.

His life.

It's all there but hidden behind a wall of

blurred recollection. As if viewing memories through a wet cloth. Shapes and images play and dance in the bright spots of his mind. Moments with the strongest feelings attached shine the brightest, but they are all held back by something that cannot be described.

Kate had a drink with him.

They worked together.

They cared for one another.

They did this silly little thing ever since they met at a bar. Strike that. In a restaurant they both worked in. A nice steak joint in the city. They'd throw back a drink then she'd go through a ritual of sorts. One that always made him smile. The same routine Murphy has been viewing in his mind but couldn't place who it was. It was him all along. At least a part of him.

Lady Brubaker did that *silly little thing*.

Performed that wonderful, silly thing to perfection.

Then she smiled as she plunged a steel blade into his stomach.

Murphy's vision slips in and out. His loose grip on consciousness is fumbling away as his blood spills out from him. He watches the dots drop, peppering the hotel carpet like a slow red rain. He needs to get to the phone that's sitting on the bed. It's like the room has stretched a mile long, the bed on the other side of the world.

She asked, *Is Murphy just like you?*

Like who?

Another name screams through the raging riot.

They called him *Noah.*

Those muscle boys from the false street fight Dr. Peyton and Thompson put him through.

Was that a glitch?

A chemical hangover from the neural chokehold they put on me?

Did they slip up or did they not know? Was their process rushed by circumstance or by the master they served? Was his name so deeply entrenched in his mind that it could not be taken away as easily as the rest? A name. A person's sense of self is so strongly attached to letters strung together to form a name that a mind cannot let it go.

No matter the abuse.

His mind held on so tightly to those memories.

A mind that wasn't ready to give up on everything contained inside of it. Everything they've told him is now up for debate. Always was, but now more than ever. Dr. Peyton and Thompson left out some major parts to this story.

Her name was *Kate.*

They call her Lady Brubaker.

His name was *Noah.*

Murphy's kinder, gentler Mr. Nice Guy half.

Did they do the same to her as they did to him?

As they were leaving the hotel bar after Peyton and Murphy were talking in the booth, Peyton said something as Thompson was rushing them out the door. She said something about Murphy's mind viewing as a third party.

Was Murphy watching the memories of Noah?

A spectator in the theater of the shared mind?

Had his mind become so mixed that Murphy watches Noah's life?

He has to move. Has to keep going.

Murphy's bloody hands slip along the leather arms of the chair struggling to push himself up. Legs feel like concrete. He fights his way to the bed. As he drops to the mattress, he sees his knife on the floor by the chair.

"Shit." Should have grabbed that.

They have a past together. Noah and Kate. A good one. He can feel it. She's something different now. Whatever she is, whatever they've done to her, whoever did it, she's not the Kate that Noah knew.

But, to be fair, he's not the Noah she knew either.

Were they merely friends?

Doubtful.

They were married. He can feel it.

A sharp pain rockets from his wound as he tries to sit up. He closes his eyes as he lies back down. A vision from inside a car screams through his brain once again.

Spinning. Flipping.

The sounds of metal crunching. The helplessness. There's a scrap of steel stuck in the driver's stomach. Much like Lady Brubaker's knife. The sights, the smells, the fear from the wreck flood his mind.

There's a gnawing. A teeth-tearing feeling of something missing.

Something forgotten.

It grates along the inside of his skull. He's missing something. Something is slipping away from his grasp. There is something out there he can't completely access. Knows that it carries an immeasurable emotional weight. His heart speeds up. Anger bubbles. Anger at himself for not being able to remember. It's on the tip of his tongue. Out there on the edge of his memory. Distant, but standing alone waiting for him.

The frustration is crushing.

What does she want?

He wants to claw at his own flesh. Scream until his throat bleeds. There's something else beyond just Kate and Noah. And it feels like everything.

"Oh my God."

His heart drops.

Blood tears roll.

"The girls."

CHAPTER 26

KATE AND NOAH HAVE CHILDREN.

Two girls.

Twins, perhaps.

There's an absence of clarity—as with everything in his mind—but there's this feeling. One that has real teeth. Sharp and tearing, fading into a free fall of loss.

The girls.

Twins.

Feels so true. So real. So correct. So much so, the hurt is strangely like home. Like it should be a part of him. These are Mr. Nice Guy's children. Noah's, not Murphy's, but Murphy feels it all tear through him. The loss. The space torn open inside. They share the weight of this emptiness.

He searches out their faces.

He can't find them.

How is that possible?

He knows they are in his thoughts. Somewhere. Buried beneath all the damage. Murphy's heart rate escalates. An unmeasurable panic sets in. The kind that can only come from not remembering your children's faces.

Murphy's thoughts step aside.

Yielding, letting Noah look for his children.

Staying out of the way as Mr. Nice Guy desperately searches for Noah and Kate's girls among the smoldering wreckage of memory and thought they share.

For the first time, there's an understanding of sorts reached between them. An agreement between Murphy and the part of him known as Mr. Nice Guy. Boundaries being set between Murphy and the man he now knows as Noah.

Mental exhaustion is setting in.

Losing blood isn't helping.

He's got to get out of here. Needs to stay alive. If for no other reason to find Lady Brubaker. Live long enough to find out how much Kate is in there. Find out what she knows. What she knows about the girls. What she remembers. What's behind those wild eyes.

He holds his wound.

The pain is unbearable.

Not enough to stop Murphy from doing what needs to be done.

Fumbling for the phone, he slip-taps his bloody

finger on the glass screen. It does nothing. The glass can't register his touch through the blood. He wipes his finger clean as best he can on the sheets, then tries again. The phone calls one of the few numbers it knows. The few it has been assigned. The rings seem to drone on forever.

The ringing stops.

A long pause, then finally, a breath.

"Tell me something good," Thompson says.

Murphy wants to scream. Wants to beat some answers out of them. Wants to cut Thompson up into thick chunks for all the lies he's told him. All the lies *they've* told him.

More than anything, he wants to drop the bomb. Wishes he could see their faces when he tells them what he's uncovered.

That he's discovered Thompson and Dr. Peyton are completely full of shit. Explain that he's sure Lady Brubaker holds his wife's personality inside her sexy, crazy-ass head. Hard for him to believe considering how they so calmly, coldly explained that Murphy was the one. *The alpha*, they said. The only mind used to blend with all of them.

How is that, motherfuckers?

Murphy takes a beat.

Considers. Goes with...

"Slight issue." Murphy coughs.

"What?"

Murphy struggles to find some stability inside his swirling mind. Holds on to what he's learned. Back pocket that information. Multiple reasons—leverage and so on—but right now he wants to make sure they send someone to help him.

If he tells Thompson what he knows, they very well might leave him to die in this Baghdad hotel room. Let that particular piece of information die off in a foreign land and go with whatever they have next up as Plan B.

Or send someone to his room to finish the job.

Just to make sure that info goes away with a bullet in the brain.

"She got away." Murphy resets, pressing down on his seeping wound. "She stabbed the shit out of me before she bounced. If that helps."

Pause on the other end of the line.

The room seems to tilt.

Pushing himself up on his elbows, he strains to get himself back up onto his feet. He knows he needs to get a towel and get some pressure on this wound or he'll pass out from the blood loss. It'll take some time to bleed out completely, but if he taps out unconscious, then all bets on his survival are off.

"Where are you?" Thompson asks.

"The hotel. In my room. In bed, thinking of you." Presses his wound. "Touching myself."

Couldn't resist. Too easy.

Murphy's not sure he would have said that. Likes it, but would never have gone that way. Noah giggles between the crying.

Another pause.

"Did she tell you anything?" Thompson asks. "Give you any information that—"

"Before she stabbed me?" Murphy's suspicions validated. "No. Surprisingly tight lipped."

They want to know what I know.

They want assurances before they bring me in.

They will kill him if they think he knows more than he needs to, or if they think his emotions have been compromised. They'll think he can be manipulated. His mind is delicate, to say the least.

A state they put him in.

These things they know all too well. They want to know everything that is floating around his busted brain. Not to mention, Dr. Peyton wants to unpack all that her little science project has to offer her. Murphy is her lost ark. A platinum drive of data she wants to plug into more than anything on the planet.

"Hello?" Murphy looks to the phone.

Dead air.

The call dropped.

He goes numb as a cold truth hits him—they will leave him here to die.

Or they just sent someone in. Someone or

someones are on the way to make sure he dies. His teeth grind hard as he turns on the balls of his feet, almost falling to the floor. The pain is immediate. A burning bite.

His knife isn't far away. On the floor, by the chair. His hands slap the wall then the dresser as he holds on for dear life. Bloody handprints now decorate the once lab-white room.

Just got to get across the room, man.

If people are coming for him, he'll need that blade in the worst kind of way. As far as pressure on the wound, his fingers will have to work for now. Picking up the knife, he slips it back behind his back.

He braces himself. Finds some form of center, then works his way back across the room following the broken streak of crimson smears along the wall. A guide for his journey to the bathroom.

As he passes the bed, he tosses his suit jacket, removes his tie. With shaking, blood-soaked fingers, he unbuttons his shirt pulling it free from the sweat of his body. The wound is small, only an inch or two. Not in the worst spot—not that there's a good one.

He thinks of the scrap of metal in the stomach from the car wreck.

His eyes close tight.

Picks away at the memory.

Something occurs to him for the first time. The multiple times he's seen that vision—that scene of the car wreck—this is the first time he's truly seeing it. He can place the face of the man at the bar. The part of him called Noah. Only now does he realize the truth of what has been playing in his mind.

Noah was driving the car.

The scene plays. The car rolls. The seatbelts give. Kate thrown free from the car. His wife is launched out from the window. The heart-stopping panic. The pain.

Metal plunges into his stomach.

Bones break and splinter inside of him. The taste of blood. It is all so vivid now.

A bright light fires off inside his mind. Like a blinding spotlight from the dark.

His eyes open wide.

His breathing pulls in and out. Heavy and deep. He's uncovered something inside his broken brain. Something has unlocked. Something it was hiding away from him. Perhaps protecting him from. Just now, while he was thinking of the wreck, his thoughts got too close and his mind had a shut-down. That bright light shut him down. Defensive measures, of sorts. As if it's all too much for him to see right now.

His vision fades, drifting into a blur, then comes back into clear focus.

He looks to the mirror.

The first time he's truly seen himself through the prism of his altered brain.

His eyes—Noah's eyes—zero in on the tats.

He knows each of them has a story. Mystified, not knowing what those stories are. Except one. There's one he knows all too damn well.

"Eat shit," he tells the devil tat.

Unnecessary feelings need to be neutralized. Push down thoughts about the girls. Kate. Lady Brubaker.

Noah needs to compartmentalize.

Murphy needs to go to work.

He jams a small towel between his teeth, then grabs the bottle of whiskey.

This will suck.

Without a moment of pause, he pours the whiskey down his stomach. Lets it roll over his open wound. His teeth dig into the towel. Pit bull hard. Blood tears stream from the corners of his eyes. Murphy and Noah together, sharing in the pain.

A searing burn spreads inside and out of his body. He grabs another towel. His entire body shakes, twitching as he dabs at the wound cleaning it the best he can. Sweat beads along his forehead. Spit drips from the corners of his lips. He sucks in a deep breath. Bites down on the towel once more.

Pours again.

The burn hits even harder this time. He fights the urge to yell. Only tiny grunts and massive profanity seep through the towel. He blots the wound once more. Looking in the mirror, he sees it's slowed the bleeding, somewhat at least. Far from perfect, but it'll buy him some time. Whiskey might damage some exposed tissue—he knows he needs real medical attention—but this will get him out of the hotel.

Maybe.

The door flies open.

Murphy spins, barely able to stay upright, jamming his right palm on the counter for stability. He pulls the knife with his free hand, pointing it the best he can at the coming threat.

"Please. Join the fun," he tells the shadows.

The heart-eating woman smiles as she leans in the doorway.

"Wow. Didn't see this coming, but I'm so happy you decided to run with your feelings. I felt the electricity too. The bed's a mess—so much blood—but we can work around it." Murphy cough-laughs. Doesn't recall always being this quick with a joke. Is Noah a wiseass? "It's been a strange evening."

She nods, then snaps her wrist as if flinging a tiny frisbee.

An injector sticks in his chest.

Another one lands below his jawline.

"That's disappointing." His tongue grows fat.

Warmth spreads throughout his body. Knees feel like soup.

Murphy slips into the void.

CHAPTER 27

FLOATING.

Untethered.

Comfortable and comforting.

As if Murphy has slid into a porcelain chamber filled with warm honey and bourbon. His mind skips and stops. Frames roll by like strips of memories from both of his lives loaded on reels of an ancient movie projector. He can even hear the clatter of the machine as the images flicker.

Noah was in the room when the girls were born on a Tuesday morning.

Murphy was in the room when they took his mother to prison on a Wednesday evening.

They said he was safe.

Kate and Noah had a small wedding in a barn converted for the ceremony.

Murphy executes a Russian informant in an alley.

He's a remarkably skilled killer, they said.

Voices are calling out on either side of him. Outside the walls of his mind, hard words are being barked.

It's all jumbled.

Difficult to decipher, but the shouting pulls him back to the here and now. Sounds like they are coming from another place. Almost another world.

One familiar voice knifes through the fog. It's the heart-eating woman's voice. She's ordering people to move their asses. Ah, heart-eating woman. She's the best.

Markus Murphy will make you hurt. Hurt is the answer to the question.

Noah wants to make everything okay. Humor hides the hurt.

We need your violence... measured and when appropriate, they said.

There's a rush of night air blowing across him. Bumps rise like soldiers across his bare chest and arms. His eyes open for a split second. Long enough to see stars pass, along with the familiar lights from outside the hotel. He smells that wonderful scent of grilled meat. Angry that he missed dinner.

He's being moved. Fast. Past the pool. Past the courtyard. He's laid out on a stretcher of some sort. He tries to flip over to see where he's heading. There's a large SUV up ahead with doors wide open. Hands push him back into place. His sight slides into its familiar fuzz once again.

Thoughts drift.

Murphy shoots three people. He moves like a demon possessed. One after the other bodies drop to the beach house floor. The wind blows through the open windows.

Murphy's mother screams at him.

They held her captive for days. They took his mother because of him.

He'd been searching for her.

He'd been relentless.

Brutal.

He's pushed into the back of the SUV. Doors slam shut. A needle plunges into his arm. A hand grabs his face as they shove a tube up his nostrils. Breathing immediately becomes easier. The thick fog clears as the pain dulls. Pushed into the background like an annoying child. People are talking all around him, but nothing makes any sense. A garble of nouns, verbs, and adjectives.

Murphy remembers the sound the steel made when they slammed his cell shut.

He remembers a fed in a blue suit telling him he and his mother would die in prison.

Murphy remembers wanting to cut that fed wide open and warm his hands in the wound.

He forces his eyes open again.

Through the window is a rolling smear that

resembles the Baghdad he saw earlier. The SUV is speeding away from the resort toward some unknown location. Unknown to Murphy, at least.

Murphy feels every bump from the back of the vehicle. Someone places their hands on his shoulders, bracing him, holding him in place. Perhaps attempting to restrain him. He thinks of wrapping his hands around their throat but can't.

Another needle punctures his skin.

Kate and Noah were in a car wreck.

Heading back home to their twin girls after work.

They were going to "play" after the sitter left.

Cold fingers inspect his stomach. Like an unsolicited medical exam from strangers. There's pressure, pulling, tugging near the knife wound but there's no pain.

Murphy killed a lot of people to get his mother back.

Did a lot of things he's neither proud nor ashamed of.

He'd do a lot more to get her out of prison.

Even through the haze of medication, his teeth grind as his mind unspools. Jumping back and forth between the split. A single mind fighting a war between Murphy and Noah.

The SUV stops.

Hands take hold of him, pulling, lifting him up, taking him out into the night. The cool air feels amazing. He wants to open his eyes, but every signal his mind sends out seems to fail.

A whiff of fuel, the sound of whirling engines informs him he's at the airport. On the runway. Guesses he's near the plane that brought him here. Makes sense. *They* think of everything. Well, not everything. Didn't count on this shitshow.

Noah wants to understand why.

Murphy wants to drink.

The cool leather of the plane's seats seem familiar. Cabin smells of recycled air. He's being leaned back as far as the seat will allow. His wound is being bandaged. He can feel the pull and tug in his skin as he shifts from side to side.

Guesses they used combat medic techniques on him. Murphy knows them well. No frills. Meatball fast and effective. The more drops of blood you can hang on to, the better. Fingers press on his neck, checking his pulse.

He's feeling a little more alert now.

The heart-eating agent is talking to a man a few feet from him. Looks like a doctor. An asshole, but probably a doctor.

The pilot opens the door, joining the conversation. Everyone looks in his direction then turns back to one another. A screen in the corner of the plane's main cabin shows the news. His now favorite news program plays. British guy in a suit surrounded by nodding heads. More about riots.

Pockets of violence sparking in different cities. *Cash Clash. Snobs versus Slobs.*

A blur screams into the plane.

She is hostile and efficient.

The heart-eating agent drops to the floor. The doctor falls back, bouncing off the wall.

Lady Brubaker puts a gun between the pilot's eyes. She hands him a piece of paper then jams a roll of cash into his chest. The pilot returns to the cockpit.

She twirls her gun in the air.

Two men move in.

Murphy vaguely recognizes their faces. They were in the escape video, maybe. Friends of Brubaker, without question. The men bind the hands and feet of the doctor and the heart-eating agent, then drag them thrashing out from the plane.

Lady Brubaker leans over Murphy.

"So." Plays with his hair, speaks soft and gentle. "We've got some stuff to talk about."

CHAPTER 28

MURPHY'S EYES OPEN WIDE.

Lids flutter like butterfly wings.

Slow to a blink, working, seeking moisture.

Same, but this time, it's different. Very different. This time Murphy is on a plane headed to God knows where.

Lady Brubaker sits across from him and gives him a finger-curl wave.

Words escape Murphy.

What does one say at a moment like this? There's no playbook here. There's only one person on the planet who knows what he's going through. And, unfortunately, it is her.

This Lady Brubaker.

Part psychopath.

Perhaps part Kate. Deep down he knows. Knows there's no *perhaps* about it.

He looks to her.

She at him. She too seems lost for words.

"Hi." Only thing he can think of.

"Hello." She smiles at the effort.

They blink. Beats crawl. Only the hum of the engines fills the tension between them. His wound pulses as he stares blankly. They share so much. So much to say to one another and no way in hell to say any of it.

He keeps running through the situation, trying to find a shred of logic. But he keeps slamming into one fact he cannot overcome. Inside this woman—this Lady Brubaker—is another woman.

One he loves dearly. Well, at least a part of him loves part of her dearly.

Sense. An abstract concept. Something others might experience. The idea of the world making any kind of sense to him from here on out is a joke. The rest of the world might turn to religion for answers. Science might hold some comfort for others. Endless entertainment content coupled with endless supplies of tasty fat helps numb the brutal truths of the world for most.

No easy answers, he thinks, *not for us.*

Us?

The shared, unsound mind of Murphy and Noah. Lonely is something they both know. Both grew up with fathers absent and mothers that were questionable at best. Spent large chunks of their lives convincing themselves they needed nothing from anybody.

Noah learned differently, learned there is a place in the world for caring people.

Learned it from Kate.

Can Murphy learn the same?

Us.

Us indeed.

Murphy and Noah hold no answers. Not sure what questions to even ask. They can only stare at Brubaker sitting across the aisle holding that gun. Their world is now and forever trapped in slippery chaos. Amen.

Nice Guy Noah wants to reach out and hold her.

Wants to tell her everything will be okay.

Murphy has serious doubts.

"What are you going to do?" he asks.

"Well." She plops a cherry lollipop in her mouth. "You're going to take this plane back to New York. But first, you are going to drop me off. Me and my boys are only hitching a ride."

"Oh, where to?"

"Not important." She sucks the lolly then shoves it in her cheek. "I don't want to be on this plane too long. It's not the company, of course. There's a good chance those frisky friends of ours might try and burn us out of the sky."

There's a cough.

More like a gag.

Murphy turns.

Sitting in the corner of the plane is a bound and gagged Eryk Pruitt. He looks far worse off than when Murphy saw him last. Sweat runs down his forehead. Face red. His eyes bulge. His arms are bound together at the forearms with tape.

One hand is heavily bandaged.

Upon closer inspection, Murphy sees the hand is not there. The arm is heavily bandaged, to be sure, but there's red seeping through the wrist. A covered stump where a hand once was. Tortured, Murphy guesses. Pruitt put up a good fight—a good fight for a tech geek god—but in the end, mean and crazy wins.

Nice Guy Noah is having a hard time processing.

Kate would never do anything like this. She wouldn't know how. Her heart wouldn't allow it.

Murphy makes a mental note.

Nothing is out of bounds with Brubaker.

"Don't worry. Your girlfriend?" She lays the lolly down on a cocktail napkin. "Talking about that hard-ass that was with you? She's okay. She's taking a nap in the trunk of a car in Baghdad. So's that doctor. Different car. Somebody will find them, once the drugs are done with them."

"Why?" sneaks out from his lips. "Why are you doing this?"

"Fairly complicated."

"I'm fairly bright."

"Not enough time, Murphy," she says. "No time to talk it all through, but..." She smiles big, thumbing toward the back of the plane. They have pulled a curtain closed, hiding the back. "I've put together a little something for us."

Murphy looks to the back.

"What?"

"Come on." She stands, extending a hand to him. "I'll help you. Think you'll like it."

Murphy looks to her hand. Open. Inviting. So many reasons to not accept it.

"Whatcha got back there?" Murphy asks, taking her hand.

"Only one way to find out."

She carefully pulls him up from his seat. Hurts like hell, no question, but not as bad as he expected. Standing pulls at the wound but he pushes through the initial surge of blinding pain. It decreases with each passing second before leveling off at *holy shit this hurts.*

He must be drowning in pain meds.

That's the only way being upright is possible.

Brubaker places his arm over her shoulder. He braces himself using a combination of her body and the plane's seats, hoping the dizziness will subside.

Walking is hard at first, but with her help, each step gets a little easier.

"Ready?" she asks, as if speaking to a child.

Murphy nods as his body goes tight.

Ready for anything.

Brubaker pulls open the curtain.

CHAPTER 29

THERE's a table with a cheap semblance of a red tablecloth spread across it.

Two plates, two soft drink cups, with a single candle between them.

The plates hold hamburgers and fries.

"Did the best I could," she says. "Not a lot to work with. Found some of it on the plane, got lucky there. Got the burgers from the hotel. Had to heat them up in the back."

Did she pick those up after she stabbed me?

What the hell?

He lets it go.

She helps Murphy into a chair, making sure he's at least somewhat comfortable. She shoos one of the men from the escape video out of the area. Murphy can only assume the other one is in the cockpit with the pilot monitoring shit.

Murphy and Brubaker are all alone now. She

spreads her hands out, showing off the table she's obviously spent some time creating. Spent some time thinking about it. Took care to get the details as close to perfect as the situation will allow.

Noah drags Murphy into a memory.

A first date.

He sees Noah and Kate.

They went to a greasy-awesome hamburger joint near campus. A true dive. A glorious college shithole. A burger joint that used candles and cheap red tablecloths as mechanisms for the delivery of charm. Noah and Kate snuck in some cheap wine—the kind with the name of a fake farm and names of fruit that don't exist on the label—pouring the crap vino into the joint's somewhat clean soft drink cups.

Brubaker fills the cup in front of Murphy's side of the table.

"With all the medication shredding through you, wine would put you in a coma." She pours herself some before taking her seat. "So, we'll have to work with grape juice. Apologies."

"I can't believe you did this." Part excited. Part anxious.

"Nice, right?"

As they dig into the burgers—Murphy is starving—he never takes his eyes off of her. More like he's studying her. Mainly her eyes. There's the sexy coldness he saw at the hotel bar, but there's something else too. He can almost see Kate behind those wild, mean green eyes.

She's back there.

He knows it.

You don't know shit, Murphy thinks.

We can help her, Noah fires back.

Brubaker snaps her fingers. "Hey, come back." She smiles. "I know there's a lot going on in there, but I need you here. Time is not endless."

"Okay." Murphy nods. "Fire away."

"Oh, almost forgot." She wipes her mouth before gently turning over his arm.

The devil tattoo is gone.

As if wiped away from his arm. Only a round, red circle of raw skin where the devil's face once was. A thin coat of ointment covers it.

"We took the liberty. Hope you're cool with that, Murphy."

"Was told that would kill me."

"I'm sure they told you a lot of things. Most of it bullshit." She tears off a bite of her burger. A pickle drops to the plate. She chews. Considers. Picks up the pickle then flings it aside. "Now, with that devil gone, they don't own you. They can't manipulate your emotions. Chemically, at least. They can't control your brain via satellites with casual swipes and taps."

"Freedom is nice, I hear."

"It is. *Thank you* are the words you're looking for."

"That's great. Just great."

"You are so welcome." She takes his blank face in her hands.

Murphy shakes her hands free, shoves some fries in his mouth.

Tastes like lukewarm heaven.

"I've given power back to you," she says. "Some at least. It may take a little while for all the chemicals to flow out of your system. We've injected you with some things that should speed up the process."

"How did you know what to give me? Was Brubaker a kindly nurse in a former life?"

"Hardly." She dismisses the question with a wave and another bite. "We dug through the files. Asked some questions of the staff and got some medical intel on their process. Asked about techniques, next steps, and whatnot."

"*Asked*? That what we're calling it now?"

"Not nice conversations. None of it pleasant." She takes his hand. "You're allowed to feel what you actually feel now. Not the feelings they choose to feed you."

"Sounds refreshing."

She scrunches her nose. "Not going to lie, this process isn't going to be pretty or smooth. Both sides of you will combine. Evolve. Grow into something—sorry, someone—new."

Murphy pulls his hand back.

She shrugs, returning to her burger.

"Not gonna be fun. Not gonna be a stroll through the park. Pretty rough ride, actually, but you will start to remember things. Truly feel those things as they become part of you. And let me be clear on something. If I'm being honest, it's gonna fucking hurt."

He can only stare back.

"Really, really bad." She takes a bite.

Neither Murphy nor Noah find words to use.

She motions for him to eat.

"I'm going to call you," she says. "I saved a number into your special little phone, the one they gave you. So now you have another number —mine. When I call you, I'm going to invite you to a location, and I'd like it if you bring Thompson and Peyton with you. If you can, of course."

She's not making a request.

This is an order, perhaps even a big-time threat.

"They're not going listen to me." He tears off a bite, wanting to keep the casual dinner conversation vibe going as long as possible.

"Oh, they'll listen. They will listen to you like never before," she says. "You'll convince them to come. Use that charm. Just get them there and they will give us what we want."

"Us? We?"

"Yes, *us* and *we*." She smirks. "You're just like us." She motions beyond the curtain. "You're like a full-on hero to the rest of my friends. You should meet them sometime."

"They say you should never meet your heroes." Murphy leans back. "I'd only disappoint."

"Doubtful. Considering you're a bit of a god to them." She checks the time. Pushes the plate away from her. "So, it's settled. I'll call you. And you bring those assholes. Okay?"

"What do they have? What do you think they're going to do?"

"Man. They did a number on you, didn't they?" Brubaker leans in, eyes wild and wide. "They are going tell us where to find them."

"*Them?*"

"Of course." She holds up her grape juice for a toast. "They are going to explain how to get our girls back."

Her words hit Murphy like a freight train.

How is it possible he's forgotten about his children, again?

How can a man forget about his girls?

Emotions flood. His ears buzz. Face burns hot.

"They have them," she says. "They've had them all along."

He can't breathe.

"Not the kind of something you can cover up with a quick joke." She tilts her head. "Is it?"

"Where are they?"

"We're going to find out."

"Kate—"

"She's here. She's listening." A tear rolls. Her lip quivers. "Never really went away."

He now knows, without a shred of doubt.

Kate is in there somewhere. He may be the only person on the planet who knows exactly what she's going through. Hurts to watch her struggle this way. Even knowing all that she's done.

"Never, ever forget that they started this. We are the victims here." She sips her juice. Wipes her eyes with her shaking hand. She takes in a deep breath, checking the time once more. "Now. I'm going to give you a little something to help you sleep the rest of the way to New York."

"Like what exactly?"

"It's called psilocybin." She smiles. "Well, a cocktail of things, but mostly psilocybin."

"Not sure I—"

"It's a psychedelic. Don't let that concern you, but it is a trip. One that I, and the rest of us, have been on. You'll start seeing colors and geometric designs. It will be cool and lovely, and then, boom. An explosion of chatter between the areas of your mind that haven't been able to communicate. It's pretty crazy shit actually."

"*Boom?*"

"Boom indeed." She downs her grape juice. "But I want to leave you with a final thought. Something for you to chew on during your little journey inside yourself. And I want you to really dig into this."

She motions toward someone behind him.

Murphy senses the two men behind him. "Wait—"

"I want you to think about that night." She's handed the syringe.

"Don't," Murphy says.

"I want you to think about the night of the car wreck."

Murphy's heart skips a beat.

He feels the sharp steel torn from the car stab into his stomach. The memory of the pain is so vivid. Alive and dancing. The same sensation when her knife plunged into his stomach at the hotel.

He can't believe it.

"Did you use pain as a marker? Did you stab me to jump-start my mind?"

"I'll let you work that out." She grins. "Pain is powerful."

He remembers driving through the country that night.

Him and her.

Kate turning on the radio. Her rubbing his shoulders.

The memory is similar, he's seen it before, but this time it's different. He's not watching someone else drive.

He's driving.

Noah and Murphy as one.

The point of view of the memory is his own. He sees the road. He can remember the feel of the wheel. The glow from the speedometer and the radio is within reach.

He can see Kate from the driver's seat.

His mind burns as he drives. There's anxiety. Worry. Guilt. Problems churn over and over grinding in his mind. Thinking of all that's wrong with their life. Money. The house is falling apart. The car held together with spit and hope. The girls.

Kate is telling him things will be okay.

Murphy is no longer a spectator in these memories. He is receiving a crash course in Kate. She's kind. Strong. Beautiful. She's everything Noah remembers Kate was. Murphy soaks in what Noah is feeling. Everything. He understands why he loves her. Who wouldn't? She's amazing in every way.

Brubaker was right.

His mind is blending, coming together as one now.

Murphy and Noah becoming singular.

"You were there," he says, barely above a whisper.

Something inside her comes unhinged. He can see it. She's no longer able to hold it back.

Brubaker's unbreakable cool is shattered. It's all in her eyes. The rage. The sorrow. It's there, as real as her thoughtful recreation of their first date.

"Correct." She nods as the tears form. "I was there. So was someone else we know."

She shoves the needle into Murphy's arm.

"Stop." Like ice-cold milk spreading, creeping through his veins.

A metallic taste coats his tongue.

He tries to get up from his chair. Pushes down hard with his hands with all he has. Strength has been reduced to nothing. All the manic power Murphy possesses rendered useless. He's shoved back down like a limp doll. The two men hold on tight, strapping his arms down to the chair. Murphy thrashes, fighting with the little he has left to throw at them.

His fists tight.

Veins pop along his neck.

Lady Brubaker looks to him. "Let your heart and soul do what they're going to do. Stop fighting yourself. But don't gloss over it either. Take it in. Let all the hurt and joy rush in, and then let it go when it's done with you." Her expression shifts, turning oddly cold as tears stream down her face. "Give your mind permission to make peace with it. All of it. I did."

"Kate," he calls out.

Murphy feels the familiar sensation of peeling away from the world.

A slide away from the here and now.

Lady Brubaker's gaze is like a funeral.

The plane begins its descent.

"See you later, guys," she says, touching his face.

CHAPTER 30

There are shapes.

Amazing colors melt into fields of light.

Pulsing emotions fill his thoughts. Wonderful feelings that words don't do justice. He's a witness to something unbelievable. Something he's never seen or felt before, yet void of the anxiety that walks hand in hand with the unknown.

He can see sounds.

He can see love embodied in color and light.

An amazing sensation of calm blankets him. One delivered from the idea that everything is okay and nothing has been or ever will be wrong again.

He feels loved.

Understood. Cared for. Then...

Boom.

The ocean breeze blows.

Feels nice, but different from where he was seconds ago.

He's always liked the taste of salt in the air. Likes sun even more as it warms his skin.

Murphy slides a black ski mask over his face. It's scratchy. Stinks of peanuts and bourbon, but it somewhat matches his black suit and electric blue tie. He loves the feel of a good suit.

Checks the load. His Glock is ready.

Green light means go.

Mother called him about a job about a week ago.

A job they could go away on, she said.

Sort of gig that sits your ass on an island drinking the good shit for the duration, she said.

A gig she needed to *get her shit right.*

That Mother, she's all right.

Always with the sugar mouth. Always the dreamer.

Murphy can't believe he used to think this way. Noah is taken back by Murphy's feelings for his mother. This wasn't present before.

But they both know it is real.

Murphy watches what he did that day. Sees himself move with purpose working his way toward a house near the beach. Hours ago, he killed three men in San Diego.

They were assholes. Such assholes.

He took one of those assholes' car, then drove up the PCH to this sleepy little beach town. After parking the stolen car behind a dumpster, he administered his crude but ultimately extremely effective device.

A little something he learned from a domestic terrorist a few years ago.

A terrorist who didn't realize Murphy was someone he couldn't trust.

Still, Murphy never missed an opportunity to learn, even from bad guys. And on that day, he learned how to make a crude device that will turn the car he stole from the assholes in San Diego into a fireball that will go off about five minutes from now.

He didn't know if he needed the diversion or not, but he knew he needed the car to go away. God knows what story that car could tell those who wanted to hear the latest tales about Markus Murphy. What paths it would lead cops and feds to.

It's a shame.

It was a nice ride.

A vintage candy apple red Porsche 911. There are maybe less than a dozen left on the planet. A gas-fueled monster designed and crafted during a time when human drivers and power were valued. Before the driverless, limp electric computers on wheels took over.

Don't get Murphy started.

In addition to helping himself to the candy

apple red Porsche, Murphy also helped himself to the drugs the assholes in San Diego had available.

Just shy of all of the drugs, if the truth is going to be told.

Reds and blues.

Yellows and polka-dotted whatever.

Snort, smoke or shoot—let the fans decide. Murphy has been dabbling in the art of self-medication for the last few years. Fancied going pro at some point. Maybe if he lives through this.

Now, Noah takes it all in.

Noah sees the memories of Murphy.

Noah is now seeing the beginning of the beach house scenes he's seen played before.

Like someone else's story is being downloaded into his thoughts. Trying Murphy's tale on for size. Feeling it. Getting used to the texture, working over the rough spots. He's soaking up Murphy's life as Murphy is soaking up his. The worst moments of both of their stories laid out for their viewing pleasure. To be seen and accepted for what they are.

Unvarnished truths.

Zero apologies requested or given.

The last person—last San Diego asshole—told Murphy he could find his mother at the beach house. That was before Murphy put two in his chest and slit his throat for good measure. Murphy had been looking for a while. Looking for Mother.

He's left a trail of dead assholes from sea to shining sea searching for his dear, sweet mother.

Mother needed this job, this gig, and deeply needed the money from it.

Endless male errors. Financial disasters. Failed jobs. Her life was a series of tragedies and mistakes. Although she'd never call them that.

Excuses and reflection are for pussies, she said.

But her life could be accurately described as a tragic mistake, if you were so bold to tell her. Murphy knew it.

Yes, Mother needed this gig to turn her past into a real-life Etch A Sketch. Shake it hard and start clean. She used to keep the ancient toy on her nightstand. She played with it—sorry, *worked* with it—all the time. Kept it next to her Bible. Next to her medicines. Next to her gun.

If he was being honest, he needed the gig too.

Needed some going away money. Wanted out of his own tragic mistakes. His thinking was getting cloudy. Thinking and feeling much more than a professional murder and mayhem machine ever should. He still enjoyed the work. The simplicity of the result. Dead or alive. Red light, green light. Still, he could use a clean life-shake as much as she could.

He knocks on the door of the beach house.

Glock held down by his side. His finger resting to the side of the trigger. Ka-Bar knife tucked behind his back. He positions himself out of the sight line of the small window by the door. He presses his thumb over the peephole, knowing there's more than likely some form of camera on him right now. Only upside to this *search and rescue op* is that escape from the house is limited. There's an open beach and endless water behind the house and a long run uphill to the main road. Not great escape options for the poor bastards in this house. Murphy is also meaner and stronger than anything inside there—except Mother, of course.

Murphy doesn't enjoy going in like this.

The Wild West style bullshit.

Not preferred.

With his day job—killing for the government nine to five—there was a plan. Always a plan. Layouts of rooms. Satellite images. Drone footage. Intelligence, with gigs of data on the people inside. Escape routes along with traffic camera video feeds establishing the pattern of things. All things were known, evaluated, and plans made beforehand. Any unknowns were unwelcome.

Sure, things went sideways.

Variables that can't be foreseen can and will pop up. An unhappy accident here and a blown operation there. AI and the biggest of data can help but the unpredictable happens when bullets fly and bodies drop. The massive universe of what, how and when is hard to predict with complete accuracy. But, to be clear, things always started with a drop of intel and then a dab of a plan.

The only plan here is to kill everyone except for Mother.

Perhaps that was Murphy's plan his entire life.

"What the fuck?" asks a gruff voice behind the beach house door.

"Like a word," Murphy chirps.

Spike of silence.

A fireball erupts. Murphy almost forgot about the sweet red Porsche parked up the hill. Smoke plumes mushroom-like up into the clear blue. Murphy removes his thumb from the peephole. A shadow shifts behind the curtain. Murphy blasts double rounds into the door. The shots boom, echo, then trail off into the ocean air. Not much to contain the rip of violence along the beach.

It's okay.

Murphy wants it loud.

Doesn't know why, perhaps the self-medication has finally dulled the edges of his usual careful killing. Regardless, he wants it loud as hell.

Murphy kicks in what's left of the door.

A body lies in a bloody mess a foot from where he stands. He hears his mother's scream. More like a battle cry. She's in the corner but there's not time to check her for wounds. He feels the tingle of death that's about to begin.

This is Murphy's time.

Murphy's gift.

It's as if he can see the future of his violence. He can always alter and adapt, but he knows where he's going before the kill clock starts.

Three men in the living room. Maybe more in the back.

The first one grabs a shotgun from under the couch. Murphy puts two in the sternum, then one in the face. The man's wide body crashes into the glass table behind him. Shards dance and bounce off the white tile floor. Blood seeps between the grout.

Another man grabs his phone, hauling ass toward the back of the house.

Murphy stops him.

Two in the back.

The last one in the room pulls his weapon, racing toward Mother. Murphy puts a bullet in his temple before that man can get within three feet of his mother. In the blur, between the dusty blood cloud, Murphy sees a bottle of whiskey on the floor by the couch.

She's still yelling.

Can't make out the words.

He hopes they are a call of appreciation. Of praise, perhaps.

Good job, son.

Murphy knows better.

A baseball bat cracks his shoulder. Murphy's teeth grind. He spins around, firing a single shot between the man's eyes at the closest of range. The man's body wilts, slipping, sliding onto the bloody tile below him. Murphy watches it flow. All the red. His mother barks in the background.

The ocean breeze blows through an open window.

Murphy picks up the whiskey bottle, takes a long pull.

"That's some rude shit," Mother says.

His collective mind stops.

A moment of frozen thought between Noah and Murphy.

Did we hear that right?

The bar with Kate.

Murphy sees the scene now though Noah's eyes. He is standing at the bar. Two glasses of whiskey. "That's some rude shit," Kate says with searing confidence. Her eyes. The bite of her lip.

Noah's favorite memory.

The strangeness of the memory slides away for Murphy. A connective moment between them. A fusion of thought.

Did Mother say that?

Did Kate?

A voice roars inside his head. Screaming inside his hurricane of confusion, fighting to be heard in the chaos. The throat tears, ripping off the force of the scream. He wants to wake from this. Shake free from whatever chemical cocktail Brubaker gave him.

Is this what she wanted?

Is this what was going to 'fucking hurt?'

He knows he's still on the plane.

Hopes he's still on the plane.

Murphy's thoughts slam into one another. Unable to parse them out.

Memories collide.

His eyes crack open.

He's in a dimly lit room.

A single light bulb sways, hanging down by a thick red cord. Attached to some unknown place above him as if dropped down from a pitch-black abyss that goes on forever. It's cold. Air feels electric and tight. His breath balls into clouds in front of him as he breathes in and out.

He's strapped to a steel chair dressed in a gray pinstriped suit with a pink tie.

The suit he wore in Baghdad.

Unable to speak. His mouth doesn't respond to his mind's requests. As if his lips have been stitched together with thick, hairy twine.

His mother and Brubaker are there.

Their lips do not move but he can somehow hear them.

More like murmurs. Jumbled but emotional.

They move slow, circling Murphy like sharks. Murphy fights the straps of the chair. Brubaker and his mother continue to speak to him without speaking. Their thoughts audible. Their voices are clear now.

You will be monitored constantly. You know that, right? From here on out, Brubaker says.

Your emotional state. Your mental state. We, they will be watching, Mother says.

Their tone is friendly but stern.

Cautionary yet kind. Someone who cares but isn't playing games.

Did the big bad world break you? Mother asks. *Or were you always broken?*

Most of us spend our lives in hiding. From others, Brubaker says. *From our thoughts. Hiding from everything. You? You've been hiding from yourself.*

A new sound breaks through the words of Brubaker and Mother.

A giggle.

Tiny footsteps.

Children are playing in the distance. The soft sounds of two girls laughing. His body trembles. He knows those laughs. He knows those footsteps.

His favorite sounds on the planet.

Sounds he couldn't remember. Ones he never thought he'd hear again.

Mother and Brubaker continue. Their conversation speeds up. Hard to tell who's saying what. Murphy can only do his best to listen as they continue to move round him. Talking as if he's not there.

Can Noah handle the anger?

He's seen rage before.

Seen it in his dad.

And his mother.

When his dad came home blind-drunk...

Yes?

His dad used to hurt him.

Oh yes, he knows this rage all too well.

And now he's stuck in one brain side by side with that same rage.

The car skids along the grass on its roof, cutting up the ground before slowing to a stop.

Tires spin wildly then slow into a loose wobble. Fluids pour from the hood forming puddles on the ground. Steam plumes. Stink of burnt rubber and gas. A violent silence now fills the cool night air.

Kate's body lies broken and still in the wet grass.

Noah fights to breathe as his blood spills.

He knows he's still on the plane.

He hopes he's still on the plane.

Looking down, he sees a severed scrap of steel jammed into his stomach. A level of searing pain he didn't know was possible. His thoughts fight the fog. Thoughts that are stronger than pain.

His thoughts are of the girls.

Their twin girls. The day they were born. Playing on the living room floor. How sweet they smelled fresh from their bath. How he read to them each night. How soft they were as he kissed them goodbye before leaving to go to work. Fragments of memories scream through his dying mind. Halting on a single memory of Kate. A replay of their last drink together.

Noah is present.

Murphy is there as well.

No longer a spectator.

Trapped, pinned, bleeding out in the twisted wreckage of their car. The car they hated. He hated. He wanted a better, more reliable car for his family. Right now, this is a car he'd love to have back. Murphy can feel Noah. A billion neurons firing off like a crashing meteor shower.

There's deep pain. Longing. He misses them. It's unbearable to accept. Murphy takes it all in. All the good times he spent with her, with Kate, all of it rips through his mind at blinding speed. So many great memories to absorb. So many gone by too fast.

He remembers.

Their first date, much like the one Brubaker recreated on the plane.

School together. Studying together. Helping each other with tests, papers, and presentations. Kate was so good in school. Dedicated. A work ethic Noah could only admire from afar.

Flirting at work.

Keeping it quiet because they didn't know how management would handle it.

The first time they slept together. Everything about it. Her face. Her eyes. The sounds. The taste of her. He put on some cheesy diva love songs because he thought she'd like it. The way they laughed after, relieved the first time was out of the way. A solid foundation to work from, but they knew their best was in front of them. Frustrated their bodies would force them wait, at least a few minutes. They shared without holding back. Without apologies or strategy. Honest emotions void of an agenda. Unfiltered affection.

He remembers.

The day he found out Kate was pregnant.

The excitement.

He remembers.

The fear. Fear that he wasn't ready. Fear that he wouldn't be enough.

On the day they were born, in the delivery room, Noah cried as they cried. Cried through the smiles. Tears fell as he held Kate's face in his hands. He did not understand life was capable of being like this. His heart was so full.

He remembers.

Emotions roll in waves and he lets them.

No jokes to be made.

No looking away.

The girls were the answer to the question. One he didn't know how to ask. The start of something bigger than himself. More important than him. Nothing before prepared him for that moment, and he knew nothing would ever be the same.

The memories are wonderful, and crushing.

Soothing, yet still rough and prickly to touch.

Murphy takes them in as his own. Lets them wash over him as he lies in the car's wreckage with his body failing. His chest heaves in and out. Blood fills his lungs. A new perspective on a familiar view.

A silver car stops on the highway.

Electric.

Driverless.

Noah—Murphy—the line is fading—cranes his neck to look through the shattered glass that drips with his own blood. His grip on consciousness is slipping. Through tunneled vision he sees a tall man with a buzz cut step out from the car.

Noah can't manage a single word.

Murphy cannot utter a syllable.

He begs his body to move, but it cannot. A battered soul in a broken shell.

His mind recalls this moment with perfect clarity. Playing out as if it was yesterday, yet something that was hidden before now. Now able to see this through much different eyes. He processes these horrific minutes knowing now who this tall man is.

Thompson.

Thompson was there.

Their shared mind was able to lock that away somehow.

Were Murphy's and Noah's minds working together to protect themselves from the truth?

Thompson leans his long, tall body on the roof of his car, waiting, looking over the wreckage with a calculating gaze. He works that steel toothpick between his back teeth.

Was Dr. Peyton there as well?

Murphy scratches and claws at the deepest corners of his mind but doesn't see her. Was she there that night? Questions mount. Burning like wildfire.

Did she know?

What did she know and when?

Can Murphy trust anyone? Is Brubaker the only one he can talk to?

She's never lied to me.

Thompson waits on the side of the road while studying the *accident*. Soaking up any sounds that may come. There are none. No words uttered. No signs of life seen.

Murphy bites back the pain.

Thompson turns to the right, looking over Kate's body resting in the grass about thirty yards from the knots of metal that no one could walk away from. She moves ever so slightly. A small tilt to her head. A tilted look toward the car. Her fingers grip the grass. Murphy can't believe it—*she was still alive.*

Thompson moves into the field. Closer to the car. Murphy hears him count to ten.

There are no screams. No cries of pain or terror.

"Perfect." Thompson stops, looking over the area.

Thompson glances up then waves off the bloodred light hovering just above him. Sending it cutting through the night. As if it completed a job.

"Okay." He slaps his hands together. His accent is southern and thick. "We're on a clock."

He circles his finger in the air.

A line of headlights pours over the highway speeding his way.

"Let's do this shit."

Murphy and Noah's eyes close.

"Hey, you okay?" a man's voice asks.

Murphy feels a finger tap his shoulder.

"You awake?"

His eyes crack open. He's covered in sweat. His hair soaked as if he's been wandering the streets in the rain. His heart pounds like a sledgehammer.

The man—Murphy recognizes him as the copilot—unstraps his arms.

Murphy squeezes his fists closed then opens them quickly trying to work the feeling back into them. His mouth feels dry, throat scratches like sandpaper. He smacks his lips together. On the table next to him is the makeshift date Brubaker pulled together. Murphy grabs his cup of juice, sucking it down as if it were the last bit of liquid on earth.

"I gotta get back. Wanted to check on you before we landed." The copilot thumbs beyond the curtain. "You sure you're okay?"

Murphy nods as he sits up. His head is on fire. His stomach wound hurts like hell. He almost forgot about his encounter with a knife. He feels worse and better at the same time. As if cut in half and then crudely stitched together.

"Okay." The copilot turns to leave. "Thought they killed you or something."

"Not yet," Murphy calls out. "Where'd they go?"

"We dropped them off in Beirut. You've been out awhile, man. We'll hit New York soon."

The copilot moves through the curtain.

Murphy's head is a scrambled mess. He's not even going to try to unpack all that played out in the theater of his mind while he was out. Brubaker wanted him to see it all, that much he knows.

Who's running the show in Brubaker's head?

Was Kate instructing this as well?

Trying to find a way to Noah?

Working together to create a version of Noah. Perhaps like the version of Kate she's attempting inside of Brubaker.

The girls.

Murphy wants to stop thoughts from coming.

Get out of your head, brutha.

Think.

There is only one way to the girls. To Kate. To anything that resembles your life.

Think.

Get your head right or this will run us over.

Beirut makes sense.

Brubaker and her buddies can work their way through Turkey. Maybe catch, or force, a ride to London or Germany. Maybe Romania. From there, they'd be clear to go wherever the hell they want. He's sure Brubaker is former military, or CIA, or whatever, but she would know how to move around the globe.

Murphy knows damn well where they're headed.

Only one place Brubaker wants to go.

New York.

No way she will call him from anywhere else on the planet. She is on a clock. Working a plan. She wants him to bring Peyton and Thompson to a place of her choosing. She wanted him to remember. Wanted him to know what Thompson and Peyton have truly done.

To him.

To them.

The wheels skid, screeching as the plane touches down.

Noah doesn't know what to do.

Murphy knows exactly what to do.

CHAPTER 31

Murphy waits for the elevator to reach the roof.

Shoulders raised up tight.

Foot tapping like a machine gun.

Lusting to be cut loose.

Peyton and Thompson wanted to meet somewhere where eyes wouldn't be on them. This apartment building fits the bill. A once luxury living destination that isn't what it used to be. The nosedive to the economy has made it hard to rent a place like this. A ripped sticker clings by the numbered buttons telling passengers to vote for Biden. Another message urges them to make America great again. Still, far nicer than any place Murphy or Noah grew up in.

He knows this building.

Remembers it well.

Knows it was constructed shortly after the 1929 market crash. Heard it was, at one time, home to famous mobsters Lucky Luciano and Frank Costello. Murphy knows he personally kicked the shit out of some mobbed-up guys here once. Maybe about a year ago. Maybe longer. The brain is working its way back online, but things are still hazy and out of reach. Dates and times are difficult to assign. Both minds fight for equal time. Thinking for two.

He attaches a suppressor to his Glock.

Murphy raged off the plane from Baghdad and then into a car they had waiting for him. Very kind of Peyton and Thompson. Noah tried to calm himself down. To reason with Murphy. Tried to present a case for rational conversation. A *let's hear them out* style of meeting instead of what Murphy is thinking. Murphy only heard the buzzing of a fly. Noah's words were doomed from the start.

Dim numbers light as he passes each floor.

Each ding thunders like a big bass drum in his ears. One after another. He clinches his fists tighter and tighter. His nails dig into his skin. Muscles vibrate. Part from excitement. Part from fear.

The final ding booms.

Rooftop reached.

Doors open. The tunnel vision of a killing machine takes over. Murphy explodes out of the elevator. Hasn't felt this alive in days.

Confident. Mad. Ready.

Shafts of light from the setting sun carve up the

rooftop. Oranges blend into reds and blues with smears of purple filling the gaps.

The roof is open, and empty. The damp stink of the city below is ever present. A chilling bite of wind kicks up, working its way over and through his body. Murphy barely notices. His body heats like a furnace.

Moving quick.

A march with extreme purpose.

He shakes his shoulders, keeping the grip on his Glock loose but in control. Sets his jaw. Sounds from the protests below thump a muted cry. Muffled, but their anger can still be heard even from this height. Central Park sits just over the edge of the building.

Peyton and Thompson stand toward the park side of the roof.

They turn as Murphy storms their way. Peyton grips her tablet tight.

Thompson holds on tight to his arrogance.

Murphy burns white hot, unable to mask his state of mind.

Doesn't want to.

Thompson looks to the gun in Murphy's hand. Instant recognition of the unmistakable violent energy moving his way.

Thompson reaches for his gun.

Murphy twist-snaps Thompson's wrist without hesitation. Thompson's gun slips loose from his grip. Murphy takes the knee. The crunch of bone, the dull pop of ligaments echoes, spreading out along the empty roof.

Thompson lands hard on his back. Face twisted in pain.

Murphy kicks his gun away, sending it skidding out of reach. Peyton takes a step back. Face frozen. Hand moving toward her screen.

"Don't." Murphy's finger is in her face. "Do not do a damn thing."

Murphy stands over Thompson. Watches him hold his knee with his only functioning hand. Spit flies from Thompson's lips as he tries to communicate through the pain. Murphy raises his gun. Communication is a waste of time.

Easy.

Don't redline just yet.

"You killed them." Murphy crouches down, wrapping his hand around Thompson's throat while jamming his gun to Thompson's forehead. "Go ahead, lie to me. Tell me you didn't."

Fuck easy.

Blew past the redline hours ago.

"Who?" Peyton's expression drops.

Murphy keeps his eyes on her. Watching, closely noting her responses.

"Not a clue what you're babbling about, boss," Thompson coughs out.

"I'll clarify." Murphy leans in, inches from his

face. "You killed Noah and Kate. They were alive after the crash. You could have gotten them help."

"You're crazy." He turns to Peyton. "He's crazy."

"No shit." Murphy regrips his gun. "You didn't even try to help them. Chose not to bother, not part of your agenda. You drained what was left of their minds before they died, then wheeled them in as your CIA sponsored experiment. Big winner from your talent search, right? You fucking piece of shit."

"What is he talking about?" Peyton asks.

"He's insane. You know this. He's out of his damn tree."

"They were perfect. No real family. Both military. They had something to tap into. Easier, simpler to connect minds with some common ground to string together, right? Murphy and Noah. Lady Brubaker and Kate." Murphy stands, pulling Thompson up with him. "Who was Brubaker? Government sponsored murder queen? Wait, let me take a swing at it. Contract killer who played the part of a high-end call girl to bring in men that needed to die. Close?"

"Wait... wait. Please. Stop." Peyton steps in. "Lady Brubaker was assimilated with you." She turns to Thompson. "Murphy was the only alpha profile used. Who is Kate?"

Murphy studies Peyton's face.

Watches every move.

He reads her confused, frightened expression. Lost and reeling. Murphy can see her eyes drifting. Her buzzing mind trying to break down what she's hearing. Working overtime to understand the unthinkable.

"You said..." Peyton swallows. "You said you mapped Noah's thoughts, then he died in the hospital. You never said anything about—"

"Peyton." Thompson shakes his head. "I don't know what the hell he's talking about. He's gone full-on psycho. You knew there was a high probability of meltdown." He motions to her tablet. "Pop his top. Now, before he—"

"Murphy and Brubaker, they probably had a common ground too. Sound logical? Rational?" He's talking to Peyton as much as Thompson. "Explain. Talk to me like I'm five." Murphy searches her eyes for the slightest hint of bullshit while he rants. "Brubaker is around the same age as Murphy. Probably in training around the same time. Probably the same place, but never met. Tell me I'm way off on this."

"Oh my God." Peyton is reeling. She begins pacing. "They couldn't match the personalities between the sexes. Too much biological difference to overcome, no matter the similarities. The baselines would be way off." She stops. Her eyes dance. "Holy shit. How did I miss that? They must have discovered it during their trials. They had the alpha; they had the killer they wanted, but they also didn't want to be limited to only males." She nods ever so slightly, processing as she speaks. "They probably tried, but they didn't synch up. We only worked with Murphy or our side. They needed a female. They found a new alpha in Brubaker."

She locks eyes with Thompson.

"Tell me that's not true."

"Peyton..." Thompson scrambles for something, anything to say.

"Also needed a stable female mind to match with Brubaker. You must have thought you hit the jackpot when you found Noah and Kate." Murphy presses the gun harder to Thompson's head. "You killed them both. You mixed my mind up, lied to me, then hoped like hell that my battered brain would never connect the dots. Never once thinking that she would lead an uprising and bolt. That she and I would chat over hamburgers."

"Thompson. Please, tell me he's wrong," Peyton pleads.

"Look." Thompson turns to Peyton, Murphy's gun still pressed between his eyes. "This was never going to work if we continued down the path we were on."

Peyton stumbles back, her hand over her mouth.

The truth slams into her.

"Your work needed to be escalated," Thompson says. "You deserved to see it come to life."

"Don't." She barely gets it out.

"Peyton." Thompson fights to reason with her. "Someone had to do what needed to be done. The needs of the project were too damn specific."

"I can't believe you."

She's so angry she's vibrating.

Murphy pulls the gun back from Thompson's head.

"Oh please." Thompson waves his one good hand, dismissing her shock. "You know damn well that we couldn't have a living subject. Now way to cover all that up. What if they talked? What if they told their story to the entire world?"

"No," Peyton says. "We could have done something—"

"You would have been waiting years for the perfect people to conveniently die of natural causes exactly when you needed them to. It may never have happened. The reality of it all is ugly as hell. You set an impossible task of finding the right subjects with a list of qualifying criteria a mile long. I did what I had to do for all concerned. And yes, that includes me. But don't deny this worked... on a certain level. Your dream worked, Dr. Peyton. The scientific implications of this are endless. You did it." Thompson holds his arms out wide. "You're welcome."

"So... he's right?" Peyton's eyes go blank. "They were alive?"

"It had to go that way. Those people—" Thompson says.

"They've got names, motherfucker." Hair on the back of Murphy's neck stands up straight.

"Tap the screen, Peyton. End this and we can start over. We learned so much from what's happened. We can do better." Thompson's face is red. His words race. "Listen to me. Those two were headed down a dead-end life. You should have seen the way they lived. That house they lived in. Buried neck deep in unpayable debt, shit jobs they were going to lose. Seconds away from homeless. We gave them an opportunity. To do something with their lives. Be part of history."

Murphy knew what he was going to do before he even got off the plane.

Just needed to see her face as he asked the questions.

"I can't believe this." Peyton wraps her face in her hands.

"I spared them. That life was headed straight to shit."

Murphy pulls the trigger.

Not sure which side gave the order.

CHAPTER 32

A WHISPERED zip tears through Thompson's head.

His body goes limp, flopping down in front of them.

Red mist drifts, disappearing into the cool air.

Peyton wilts. Her eyes wide. Mouth open yet unable to scream.

She looks to Murphy. Finger raised about to tap.

Murphy turns his gun on her.

"Don't." He shows her his forearm where the devil once lived. "It's not going to do what you think."

Her body shakes. Her control is all but gone.

Almost.

They both know she can still blow out the back of his skull with the touch of her skin on a glass screen. Murphy knows he is still her only source of data. The only living thing that can tell her about her life's work. He also knows that will only take him so far.

"What have you done?" she asks.

"What does it look like?"

"This isn't happening. What the hell—"

"Think you told me once—*There are a lot of things we're about to explain. They will seem very strange and we understand completely.*" Murphy clucks his tongue. "Now. The *we* in this discussion, the one we're having at this moment, is your buddy Murphy and his brain-bro Noah."

He now puts the gun between her eyes.

"Got only one thing to ask you." Murphy needs to be sure. "Did you know?"

"No." Peyton trembles, barely scrapes out the answer.

"Did you know?" He presses the gun to her head.

"No, Murphy." Her eyes are full. She wipes them clear. Not willing to cry. "I didn't know what he did. I'm sorry any of that happened. I can't believe I'm a part of it."

His phone buzzes.

He lowers his gun, replacing it with a raised finger as if politely asking for a moment.

"It's her," he says.

"Who? Brubaker?"

He nods as he answers. The call only lasts a second, maybe two.

"We're going to meet her." He thumbs toward the edge of the roof. "Down there. In the park."

"Are you insane?"

"Pretty sure you know the answer to that."

"I'm not going anywhere," she barks, searching for control. "No way in hell."

"You are, and you will." He smiles. "This is how this is going to go, Dr. Peyton. You get to be my personal genie. You're going to grant me wishes —a shit-ton more than three—and if you do not, I'm going to cut the people you care about most into chunks."

She freezes.

"But let's not dwell on the unpleasant part of who I am, okay?"

"Murphy—"

"Noah is who you should speaking with."

"The timer... the eye scan. Thompson has to check in with a biometric ID. If he doesn't perform the scan—"

Murphy snaps his fingers as if remembering something important.

"Oh, you mean the explosive you stuck in the back of my head?"

She nods.

"Yeah, took a real risk with that headshot on Thompson there. One nervous bitch-twitch on his part and this could've gone really bad." Murphy pulls his Ka-Bar, handing it to Peyton. "Number uno on my wish list."

"What's this for?" She stares at his knife.

"You're gonna need a baggie or something too."

"For what?"

"His eyes, Dr. Peyton. Like you said, we need Thompson to scan in."

Peyton's face drains white.

"You can't carry them around barehanded," Murphy says. "That's gross."

CHAPTER 33

The park feels like a pressure cooker.

People packed together.

Side by side.

Anger transferred person to person. Growing, seeping, spreading throughout the park. Throughout the city and the country. Each person nurtures their own anger, feeds on it, then passes it down.

People shove and pull at one another. They shout with faces bloodred. Feels like anything can happen, as if Central Park rests on a giant pile of dry leaves waiting for a match. Looking to spark endless disturbing possibilities.

Faces void of hope.

A concert for the lost and disenfranchised.

Police do their best to keep it in check. Outnumbered as hell, but they hold the line. Helicopters circle above the swelling masses below.

Mounted officers stand at the ready. Police dogs on tight leashes. A tactical team in full riot gear is at the ready if needed.

The media swarms.

Beautiful television personalities posing as news fight for ground among the common folk. Microphones ready and willing to hear the truth. Or at least a juicy, tasty soundbite. Something to share with those at home who think they care. Chants echo and roll out among the crowd. Signs sway back and forth among the faces locked in rage. Screaming, straining for someone to hear them.

All walks are here. Every race. Every religion. Every way of life.

Together but fragmented.

Pieces of a pissed off society thinly held together by the need to release it all.

Murphy and Peyton cut their way through the masses the best they can. He tried to give Peyton the important details. Hard to keep it all together. But he thinks he hit the highlights on the way over from the apartment building.

It was a bit of a fire hose of horrible, but she seemed to absorb it all. He told her about the resort. About Pruitt. About the flight back to the States. He tried to explain what happened to him while he slept on the plane.

Difficult to put into words.

He told her about the psilocybin Brubaker gave him. Peyton reluctantly acknowledged its effects and told him it was part of the process. A vital part of a careful plan that was hacked into a million pieces. Gave the caveat it was one of the final stages and it was to be administered along with intense therapy and careful supervision.

Murphy could only tell her that there was none of that shit on the plane. All he knows now is that they're meeting Lady Brubaker inside this madness.

Where is uncertain.

She will call back with the exact spot they're supposed to meet her. Murphy leads the way with his phone gripped tight in his hand. Gun tucked in his waist. Ka-Bar knife secured behind his back.

"What is she going to do?" Peyton asks.

"That I don't know."

A billion-dollar question.

Murphy keeps his focus on the path ahead. He holds his wound, trying to not remind himself he took a blade to the gut. Thinking about it is not helpful, not now. The pain meds Brubaker laid on him were top shelf. He could take a bullet or twelve and still not feel it completely.

Maybe that was the idea.

Maybe her people are on the same meds.

He makes a note to himself to aim for heads, if it comes to that.

A fight breaks out next to them. Two men shove and swing wildly at one another. Some punches connect. Some don't. It's broken up fast by a pack of cops. The men in dark blue pull them apart, securing zip ties tight behind their backs and moving them along. Murphy watches on. *This is the simmer before the boil.*

"Her people started this," Peyton says.

Murphy stays silent.

"You know that, right?" she continues. "This? This is all her work."

"She didn't start the economic shitstorm. I've seen the news between my little naps. This meltdown has been in the works for months. Years even."

"No, but she started the riots. Her and her people."

Murphy kept his thoughts about her to himself. Kept his feelings for her from Peyton. Even though he knows Peyton can guess. She probably has massive concerns about where Murphy's—and Noah's—head is regarding Lady Brubaker.

He also failed to mention the girls to Peyton.

Trust is still up for grabs.

His mind shifts to Kate. To who she is—or was.

To what they had together. To the life he had with her and the girls. It wasn't perfect, not even close, but it was theirs and there was happiness between the struggles. He thinks of what they could have again if he could reach her. If he could get to Kate inside the burning house of Brubaker.

This can be fixed.

If a human can create the problem, then a human can correct that problem.

"You're going to undo what you did." Murphy's talking more to himself than Peyton.

"What?"

A man shoves Peyton hard.

Her neck snaps back. Another man screams into her face. Murphy levels him with a flat hand strike to his throat. The man spits and coughs, spinning away, disappearing into the crowd like a scolded dog.

Peyton is shell-shocked. As if her feet have grown roots, digging into the grass of the park. Life in the lab is different than the dark, messy world. Murphy taps her on the shoulder.

"Come on." He points ahead. "Shake that shit off."

Forward movement.

Always.

"You are going to undo what you did to her," he says in her ear, straining to be heard over the crowd. "At the very least, make it better."

"Murphy, I can't do that."

"Think you can."

"I didn't do this to her."

"You opened up *this* hell. That much I do know."

"This has gone beyond my work." Peyton's voice shakes. "This isn't like rewriting a paper or repainting a room. This cannot be undone. No backspace. No delete button."

Murphy thinks of the old toy his mother kept by her bed. How she'd shake it over and over. Starting over and over. His thoughts pull tight. Like a trigger squeezing. A sudden click launching a want for wrath. It's come on so fast, he can't even reconcile where it came from.

Green means go.

Murphy grabs Dr. Peyton by the shoulders, letting his emotions run the show. His hands grip like vices. He feels the rage flow, his blood spiked with raw power.

"Stop," Peyton says.

Murphy squeezes harder.

"You're hurting my arm."

He wants to tear her into pieces.

Wants to stomp her skull into the ground. Memories flood at the speed of light.

Noah.

Kate.

The girls.

Murphy.

Something has been released inside his mind. A valve that was holding it all back. The things he saw while on the plane. Things he's only seen in flashes. They're here with him now. This is the first time he's seen these images, these scenes, play while he's out in the wild. While he's wide awake, out in the real world, not sedated or stumbling through the haze of sleep. He can see it all now.

Memories of smiles.

Thoughts of what once was.

Sorrow and loss seep into Noah and Murphy. Absorbing it together. The desire for blood. The need for revenge.

Thompson wasn't enough.

Peyton screams at him. Begging. Pleading with him. Murphy doesn't hear a word.

Blood rolls from Murphy's eyes.

The phone buzzes.

"Murphy. Please think about..." Peyton trails off.

Murphy shakes loose from his trance. His heart pounds.

The phone buzzes.

"It's her," Murphy says, tapping the screen to answer.

"Go to the rocks west of the playground," Brubaker says. "Near the bridge."

The call disconnects.

Murphy pockets the phone then takes Peyton's face in his hands.

"I'm going to make this as clear as I can." His

words are ice-cold. Deliberate. Stabbing. "You are going to fix what you've done to us. This all needs to end."

Peyton fights back the fear. Anger taking hold.

"What does that even mean?" she barks. "What does *fix* mean? Look around you."

Murphy's hands move, wrapping around her throat.

"What? Do you think I'm going to wave a wand and she'll be fine? That you'll all live happily ever after? Four of you in two heads? Tell me you're joking."

"She wants to talk to you," he says.

"Fantastic. We'll talk. Sure, that'll go well." She coughs as his fingers press tighter. "Might as well kill me now, Murphy."

"Fair enough."

Green means go.

Murphy alters his grip, places his thumbs over her eyes, pressing ever so slightly. Her hands pull at his. Slapping, clawing, fighting to get them off of her.

Murphy's sight goes white.

Murphy releases her. Stumbling back, he bounces off a protester. Peyton rubs her neck, coughing, sucking in deep breaths. He wants to reach out to her, like he wanted to at that hotel bar. Wants to tell her he's not a monster. Even though he knows the truth.

She steps back.

"Stay the hell away from me," she yells.

He hates the way she's looking at him.

She's terrified. Afraid for her life. His hand extends toward her. His fingers tremble. Peyton looks back at him, her hard expression changing ever so slightly. As if she sees a change in him. Something different about Murphy.

Tears form in his eyes.

This time, they are not blood. He resembles a helpless child who's lost in the park.

Peyton squints. Swallows hard.

"Noah?" she asks.

He nods.

A sharp pain puts Murphy down on his knees. He holds the back of his head. Peyton scrambles, scanning her tablet.

"Shit." Muttering, she swipes and taps at the screen.

The timer is ticking down.

Murphy's vision blurs. He can't hold on to a single thought. The world is tumbling away from him as if he's being shoved off a cliff. The sounds of the park's chaos around them fades into the background.

"Hold on." Peyton stands still as the eye scan validates her identity. "Stay with me, asshole."

One green check mark shows on the screen.

One red box blinks, waiting for Thompson's scan.

The crowd steps over Murphy as he falls on the ground. No one pays attention to the human being suffering in obvious pain on the grass. Peyton swats and pushes at them doing her best to keep them both from being trampled to death. She slides to her knees in the grass, hovering over him.

Murphy tastes metal. His skin is going cold.

The world is a blur beyond the tears.

He claws at the grass, pulling himself toward Peyton. Fighting to remain conscious.

Peyton digs into her bag, pulling out a plastic baggie that contains Thompson's eyes. Her hands shake as she taps and swipes at her screen again. She angles the bag and an eye for verification.

Denied.

She adjusts the eye, slipping it around in the bag and trying again.

"Hurry," Murphy spits.

Denied.

"It's not working." She looks over the screen then leans back on her knees. "Thompson installed a fail-safe."

"What?"

"If his vitals flatline, then his access ends."

Her eyes drift as the timer ticks down. Seconds left. She looks to Murphy. Murphy's body thrashes, riding the waves of pain. The seconds peel off one by one. One last time, he reaches out to her. His hand trembles, held out for her to hold.

She looks at his open, waiting hand. Something eats at her mind. An idea gnaws. She starts to speak, then stops herself. Murphy can only look back at her, helpless and alone.

"Can I trust you?" she asks.

He can only look back at her.

"Can I trust that you'll do what you know is right? That you'll stop her."

"I..." His eyes fade. "I don't know."

"Noah? We haven't met. And sorry doesn't cover it, but please..." She presses, wanting to know what's behind those eyes. "Are you there? We need you."

Murphy stares at her through the tears streaming down his face. He manages a simple, yet unmistakable nod. Peyton takes a deep breath, tosses aside the bag of Thompson's eyes, then taps and swipes feverously.

The screen scans her eyes again.

She lowers her tablet and waits, staring up at the stars popping pinholes in the night. Waiting. Hoping she made the right choice. The wrong one is too much to consider. She's removing the leash. The last thing holding back the monster.

Murphy twists in the grass. His fists filled with dirt.

The chaos of the park swirls around them.

Her phone lights up.

"This is Dr. Peyton. Yes. Echo, bravo, nine, Charlie, one, six. Yes, correct. I authorize deactivation." She nods. "Yes, again, that is correct. I know about Thompson. Just fucking do it."

She looks to Murphy.

"Come on," she whispers.

The shaking slows.

His sight slips back into focus. The buzz in his mind winds down until it's unnoticeable. The ringing in his ears starts to fade, as does the pain. Peyton reaches out her hand, meeting his, clasping fingers tight. They hold a look. He can't imagine what she's thinking.

But he's thankful for whatever it is.

"What did you do?" he asks.

"I shut it down. Never enjoyed having a bomb in my little science project's head."

"Appreciate it." He smirks. "But it does feel like a questionable decision given my—"

"Please don't make me regret it."

He nods.

"Well, okay then." Murphy pushes himself up to his knees. "You're in luck. That was one of the wishes. Still got a few more, however."

He holds her hand tight, still never forgetting who she is.

Or what she's done.

CHAPTER 34

Murphy and Peyton reach the bridge.

They stand on the grass near a walkway that leads under a slight, moss-covered stone arch. People run under, over and around the bridge. Shouts and screams echo underneath.

The tension in the park is pushing higher and higher.

A needle in the red.

It's in the air. Feels heavy. Thick. Weighted down by what's coming.

Another fight breaks out near them. Two younger boys. Too young to be this angry. Murphy places his hand on his gun but releases it as the fight dies. Once again cops break it up, taking them down then handing the boys off with their wrists bound with nylon zip ties. Police are everywhere but yet there is little sense of control to be found.

Murphy's eyes scan the area.

Searching for Lady Brubaker. She'll be with others. More than likely the two guys from the plane. Maybe more. Thompson and Peyton said they didn't know exactly how many there were. Not a comforting feeling. Murphy thinks they are probably safe in the park, but he knows he should be ready for anything.

Anxiety radiates off of Peyton. Her eyes dance.

He can almost see the thoughts firing off inside her head. She scans the area too, but in a much different way. She is searching for a way to survive. Hoping for a peaceful end.

Murphy is looking for violence.

Seeking it out. A fist looking to connect.

There's a part of Murphy that can relate to what she's feeling. Noah feels the same. None of this is easy for Mr. Nice Guy. Murphy ignores the drama. Dismisses the flare of sensitivity and focuses solely on the here and now of it. The death and the life of it.

Murphy isn't sure what outcome is best.

He hasn't given it a lot of thought. He's letting Noah handle the wants and needs of this thing. The rational side of the ledger belongs to him. Mr. Nice Guy can balance the emotions. Murphy only wants to keep the two of them—and Peyton—breathing. He's the warrior. An instrument of chaos, and make no mistake, chaos is coming.

Is Kate still in there?

Is Peyton wrong, can she be saved?

Only one way to find out—one hell of a gamble left to try.

He'd kill everyone in this park to have her back. Execute the entire city to have his family return to normal. There's nothing more in the world that he wants right now. The desire to get back to where he was, to get back what they lost. It is crushing. Go back to before the twisted metal of the car wreck. Before the breaking of their brains. He wants his damn life back.

That's all.

Is that such a ridiculous request?

His family. His wife and his girls. He wants to get back to good.

He looks to Peyton. She's terrified, but she's here.

"You made it," Lady Brubaker says.

Murphy and Peyton spin around facing her. She stands with the two men from the plane on either side of her like the good soldiers they are. They moved up on Murphy and Peyton without warning. Murphy isn't used to someone, anyone, getting the drop on him. She probably knew this. Wanted to carve out a spot of uncertainty inside his head.

A little troubling place for Brubaker to set up camp.

"Dr. Peyton." Lady Brubaker extends a hand. "We haven't been introduced formally, but I'm familiar with your work. Big fan."

Peyton shakes her hand but has no words to offer.

Murphy watches her closely.

The tingle of disaster reaches his fingertips. He studies Peyton's reaction as he did on the rooftop with Thompson. A sliver of mistrust is still there for him. Even after all that happened moments ago. His desire to have Kate return, to have the girls back in his life, that want and desire have all but erased the risk Peyton took for him. The risk she took decommissioning the explosive in his skull was ballsy—not lost on Murphy or Noah—but that's his family we're talking about.

He knows what Peyton has to gain.

He's a walking gold mine to her.

Thompson was right; the possibilities of her science are endless. The profit potential can't be measured. Murphy zeros in on Dr. Peyton's body language. Her eyes. Taking in what she's saying through her physical traits.

She stands stiff as a board staring into Brubaker's dead eyes.

Those green, beautiful, dark and empty eyes.

Murphy can't begin to understand what Peyton's thinking. How strange it must be to be surrounded by her creations. Some she didn't know existed until recently. She must be a ball of fear spinning in a puddle of wonder.

Sickened by what her life's work has become, yet excited by it.

Concerned before, sure, but to have it all face-to-face with her? That's a whole new brand of crazy. The woman Peyton's watched over and over in the horrifying escape video is here. Brubaker is alive, in the flesh and standing in front of her.

"Please." Peyton's voice breaks as she speaks. "Whatever you're doing—"

"Don't do that," Brubaker says.

"What am I—"

"I have only one question for you. And I will ask it in a moment." Brubaker turns away from her. Zeroes in on Murphy. "Where's the other one?"

"Thompson?" Murphy says. "Oh, I killed him."

Brubaker jams her tongue in her cheek, nods, then shrugs.

"How are you doing?" Brubaker asks him. "Good flight? Get some rest?"

There's a turn in Brubaker's expression.

A new light shines in her eyes. Her mannerisms changed in a snap. Murphy can't help but take a step back. Such a sudden shift. It hits him like a freight train. He can see Kate inside of her. There's not a shred of doubt in his mind.

It can't be, he thinks.

She has control over her sides?

She just turned into Kate in the blink of an eye.

The Noah inside of him wants to hold her tight. Wants to tell her they will work this out. That they can make everything the same, exactly like it was before.

The Murphy inside of him screams.

Don't let her do this to us.

She's fucking with our head, man.

Murphy is now the voice of reason.

"What did you see," Brubaker asks, "while you were sleeping on the plane? What was playing during the in-flight movie? The one in your head."

"It was a real tearjerker."

She smiles, reaches out toward his stomach. Toward his wound. He steps back, pushing her hand away on instinct.

"Hey." She holds up her hands showing she means him no harm. "Just wanted to see how it was going down there. Sorry I had to do that to you."

Peyton watches them. She seems fascinated and terrified all at the same time.

Murphy's mind flashes to Brubaker jamming the blade into his stomach, then to the bone-rattling slam of the wreck. The searing pain of steel piercing his skin. Sharp steel stabbing him in the same place on his body. Blood coating his fingers, in both memories.

"Now." Brubaker checks the time, then turns to Peyton. "That question I had for you."

Peyton's mouth goes dry.

Murphy holds his breath.

"Where are our children?" Brubaker asks. "Where are our girls?"

CHAPTER 35

She asked the question.

The only one that matters.

Brubaker asked the question about their children—*where are our girls*—as if she were asking for directions to a coffee place. As if she wasn't surrounded by the powder keg she constructed.

"What?" Dr. Peyton's heart skips a row of beats. "Who?"

"Our daughters," Brubaker says. "You know, the ones who were left without parents. Because of you."

Murphy continues studying Peyton. Her reaction to that billion-dollar question.

Did she know?

"Children? I didn't..." Peyton loses all color in her face. "You have kids? Little girls?"

She looks to Murphy. He nods a cold, solemn confirmation.

Answer truthfully, Dr. Peyton.

Truthfully and very carefully.

"Oh my God. Please listen to me," Peyton says. "I had no idea. I didn't know anything about that, nothing about the life you had. I didn't even know about Kate until less than an hour ago."

Brubaker is on her in a snap.

Rushing in like an animal on raw meat, inches from Peyton's face. Brubaker pulls a gun, shoving it into Peyton's stomach. Murphy fights the urge to pull her back. But the hurt is fresh and unresolved. What they did to him, to Kate, to their children. An exposed nerve feeling it all.

Divided by how she saved his life only minutes ago.

"Look around, Dr. Peyton." Brubaker's face is still. Raging underneath the surface. "The park is a blink away from a bonfire. I can watch it burn. Or I can snuff it out." Bounces her eyebrows. "Your call."

"I don't know anything."

Brubaker looks to the two men standing beside her. Eyes communicating between one another. The men nod in recognition then scan the area, pulling their phones. Fingers texting. Something is happening. Murphy watches them as his shoulders creep up toward his ears.

"Nothing?" Brubaker asks her.

Peyton's mouth opens, but nothing comes out.

Her eyes helpless, begging the universe for answers she does not have.

"Okay." Brubaker cocks her head. "No need to drag this out, waste everyone's time. I'll just put a bullet or six into your body, then keep looking. Somebody somewhere knows."

"Hey." Murphy steps in closer, but not too close. "You don't have to kill her. We need her."

"Not sure we do," Brubaker says.

"Look." Murphy motions around the park. "Whatever you're about to do, let's talk about it first. Before something happens that can't be undone."

"Who am I talking to?" Brubaker turns to him, searching his eyes. "Who's in there right now? I need the one with balls."

"Nobody else needs to die."

"Odd coming from the dude who just killed Thompson."

"Ya got me there." Murphy nods.

"We really going to argue about this?"

"All these people, this park, they have nothing to do with any of this. We can find the girls. You don't need to jump-start a riot to find them."

"Oh, sweetheart, a riot is only the opening act. I'm inches away from bringing down the whole fucking thing."

Brubaker moves her gun from Peyton's stomach, now placing it between Peyton's eyes.

"Wait." Murphy places his hand on his gun. "We do need her."

"You sweet on her?" Brubaker asks. "You like the bad boys, Dr. Peyton?"

Peyton's entire body shakes.

Brubaker isn't the kind who plays games. This can and will go horribly wrong if he doesn't do something.

"Hey," Murphy says, looking into her eyes. "Talk to me, Kate. You got some time for me?"

She smiles. Her eyes gloss.

"Help me do this," Brubaker says.

"I will, just not like this. I want to talk to Kate."

"This is the only thing they understand."

"I know, but—"

"Blood, aggression. It's the only language they speak."

"I want to talk to my wife."

She bites her lip. Murphy sees an opening. A shine in her eyes.

"Think, Kate. Fight to remember. Think of our life. When we met. When the girls were born. Kate would never do anything even vaguely like this."

Brubaker moves her gun, placing it between his eyes.

"If you're gonna do it, do it," he says.

Brubaker pushes the gun harder between his eyes. Her finger tightens on the trigger. Her eyes almost jumping from her head as veins pop along her neck. Murphy places his hands on the sides of the gun, holding it to his head. His eyes locked with hers.

"Kate," he whispers. "If this is what you want, then go right ahead."

She shakes her head hard.

She yanks the gun back, takes a beat, takes in a deep breath. A reset behind her eyes.

"Kate," Murphy says, relieved. "We have to—"

"Set it off." Brubaker circles her gun in the air.

The two men beside her nod.

"No." Murphy reaches out for her. Fingers grasping empty air.

Brubaker kicks Murphy in the stomach with all the hate she has.

CHAPTER 36

HER FOOT HITS LIKE A SLEDGEHAMMER.

Could have gone straight through him, if she wanted it to.

She aimed her strike right where she stabbed him.

Murphy falls to the ground. He felt a rip in his healing wound. The meds hold back some of the stampeding pain, but even through chemical numbness the agony roars. Peyton leans down, doing what she can.

The pain from Brubaker's kick triggers his mind again.

Thoughts burn.

Murphy pounds his fist to the ground over and over. Grits his teeth, working to level out his mind, balancing his mindset for the pain. Trying to find a baseline of how this will feel and then accepting it.

Craning his neck, he looks up, searching the

park through the white spots clouding his vision. Shaking his head hard knocking loose the spike of adrenaline, he looks again.

Brubaker is gone.

She can't be.

"She's not goddamn magic. Where..." he whispers. "Wait."

In the distance up ahead, he can see people being pushed aside as she cuts through the crowd. The two men follow her while on their phones.

Two phones, two calls. One man turns, looking back and to the right. There's a cop on his phone standing in the middle of the bridge looking back toward him. He's only about ten feet from Murphy and Peyton but has a raised vantage point above them.

Murphy focuses on the cop on the bridge.

Something is off. Something about him doesn't ring true.

Murphy makes a quick scan of the area.

The officers who broke up the earlier fight stand off to the side of Murphy. They have their eyes trained on the crowd. Intense focus on everyone and everything in front of them. Standing ready. Heads constantly moving, monitoring, assessing the growing unrest in the park.

The cop on the bridge is looking right at Murphy and Peyton.

His focus is singular.

"He's not a cop." Murphy pushes himself up off the ground.

"What?" Peyton helps him to his feet. "Who?"

The cop on the bridge breaks into a chilling smile. Murphy feels an odd connection to him. Something familiar. The first time he's truly looked into the face of one of them. The cop on the bridge looks dead at them. Murphy waves.

The cop drags a finger across his throat.

"No, no, no..." Murphy's words trail off as he reaches for his gun.

The cop pulls his gun, shooting a man unfortunate enough to be closest to him.

The crowd screams.

Another gunshot rings out.

It removes the head of the cop on the bridge. Sends him tumbling down, landing on the sidewalk a few feet from Murphy and Peyton. People scream. Murphy whips around, pulling his Glock. Another man—glasses, ratty hair, in a dirty T-shirt —holds a gun aimed toward the bridge where the cop was standing.

Ratty hair made a perfect headshot from a considerable distance.

Not a shot an amateur could make with a handgun. Not one an amateur could successfully pull off during the heat of the moment. That kill was planned. No question. Only a handful of people on the planet could make that shot.

Murphy could make that shot.

The insanity of the insane sacrificing one another to... *set it off*.

"This is her. This is her plan," Murphy says, somewhat impressed. "This is so Brubaker."

A part of him smiles.

A part of him does not.

There's a strange moment of calm. The park goes eerily quiet. Not for long, only lasting a blink. But it was there. A tiny pulse of peace under the stars.

Perhaps the last moment of calm they will ever know.

The volume jumps. Intensity grips tighter. The energy of violence has arrived. Police sirens wail. Lights flash like electric red and blue gumdrops popping in the night. Officers draw their weapons, screaming for peace. Ordering calm. The crowd scatters in all directions with the roar of madness rolling across the park.

More gunshots ring out.

Bullets zip from all directions. Hard to tell from where or from whom. Another officer goes down, as does another civilian. A woman's leg blows out from under her. A piñata of flesh and bone. A large man takes a shot to the shoulder, spinning like a top to the ground. A cop chokeholds a man in a suit. No way to understand who's doing what in the swarm of men and women. A tangle of bodies moving, jumping, charging, falling in every direction.

Murphy stares at it all. Stunned. Taken back to war.

Peyton grabs him by the hand, pulling him through the crowd best she can. They push and shove, fighting for every inch. Murphy snaps out of his trance.

Back in the game.

He's lost sight of Brubaker. She could be anywhere in this ocean of meat and bone. He's seen war zones worse than this. Seen better ones too. Been here before, just never like this.

A fire breaks out in a playground.

A police dog takes down a man with a baseball bat. The beast's teeth lock into his arm, thrashing back and forth. A woman pulls at the dog, only to be taken to the ground by a cop.

A bottle gets smashed over the head of another cop.

SWAT teams pour out from vans.

A madman has taken over a horse-drawn buggy. Yelling while standing up firing a gun into the air. People dive clear. Some don't make it, getting plowed down by the wheels.

Murphy knows he has to find Brubaker.

He has to find out where she is going.

Has to know if Kate is truly gone. Is she gone forever? He fights the urge to hate himself, but he can't. Furious at himself for thinking there was a chance. That there was even a possibility of salvaging the good. Foolish to try. To think he could save Kate from inside that monster.

Yet part of him will not abandon all hope.

Noah will never completely give up—ever.

Think. *She took Pruitt for a reason.*

Murphy ducks as a pipe swings past his face. He lands a gut punch before shoving the man clear. Creating a hole, a partial path, for him and Peyton to move through. Murphy's mind sets.

Anyone in their way will be removed.

How bad it hurts, that is their choice.

"She talked about taking down the country," Murphy yells to Peyton.

"Riots in Colorado, and in North Carolina." She scrolls her phone. "There's already a video of the cop shooting that man on the bridge. Social media is all over it."

Murphy considers as he grabs a construction guy by the shirt, shoving him aside.

"This is bad, but it will die down on its own." Murphy thinks as he pushes through. "The cops and military will take control, eventually."

This is shortsighted Brubaker thinking.

Guns and blood for now, but not a big-picture plan.

Kate?

Kate would have a bigger plan.

Is she feeding off what Kate brings to the party? Is Brubaker mining her for ideas, points of view?

A bullet zips past his ear. He pulls Peyton down to the ground. Multiple shots ring out. Cries of pain. They get back up on their feet. Time is at a premium. Fires now litter the park giving a flickering glow to the night. This will all spread out into the city in no time.

"There's so much," Peyton says as she scrolls her phone. Unfazed by the surrounding insanity. "Videos. Pics. Global market futures are tanking."

One big shove, she said.

She went after Pruitt. She went after the hedge fund asshole.

Not random. Curated targets.

"Did they crack that laptop I took?" Murphy asks. "Were they able to get into the email?"

"No. They're still working on it."

"Shit." Murphy lands a punch, dropping a man who charged them.

Peyton fires her palms into the chest of a screaming man with all she has. Screaming back at him until her face reaches a new shade of red.

"Here." Murphy shoves his phone in her hand. "Pictures I took of some of the emails from the hedge fund house."

More rioters charge their way.

Murphy wants to use his gun to end this quick but thinks better of it. Gunfire will draw the cops his way, or even more bullets from the random insanity of the crowd. He does not have time for that shit. He spins one woman into a hold, then plants his foot in the throat of a guy who's closing in on him. Fists fly. Bones crunch. Blood sprays.

They keep coming.

"One email about Pruitt going to Baghdad," she says, searching his pics.

"Keep looking." Murphy lands his elbow to some asshole's face. "There's one, several people on it."

"Looking."

Bullets carve up the night. Beside their feet, pops of dirt explode.

"Something about a meeting," she continues, unfazed by the blasts. "Wait... Holy shit!"

"What?" Murphy shoves a limp body aside.

"There's wrath of God names on this email. Including Pruitt, it's the heads of the three largest tech firms in the world."

"That's the one."

Murphy's mind clicks.

He thinks of Kate.

Oh my God.

He remembers how they used to study together. He helped her with a big paper she stressed about. She spent weeks on it. It had her twisted in knots.

Pouring over the data every night.

Working the numbers. The topic was how three companies were responsible for ninety percent of the stock market. The entire US—and most of the global—economy is tied to only three companies. Those three companies hold important manufacturing, distribution, or funding relationships with the vast majority of the companies around the world. If a company had any ties to those three firms, they got hurt by a downturn.

Kate had all the data.

As she always did.

When those *Mega Three* companies took a hit on anything, like missed earnings, or a sexual harassment issue with management, or any form of negative news, the overall stock market took a hit. Didn't matter if they were a tech firm or not. It was a spiral in the markets that would spread to all industries with nobody immune from the pain.

"That's it," Murphy says. "That's what she's doing."

"What?"

"She's going to crash the market. The final death blow to a reeling economy."

Violent riots plus a lighting fast, catastrophic financial meltdown.

That might do it all right.

And if that's not enough, she'll keep going.

The pieces fall in line inside his mind. One by one landing, making sense. The talking head news shows over the last few days. The takedown at the hedge fund house. Going after Pruitt. Why she didn't kill him—she needs him to get to where they're going. She tortured him.

There's a beauty to what she's doing.

Beauty in her brutal simplicity. The brutal combination of Brubaker and Kate.

"She will kill all three of them and watch the world burn," Murphy says.

"They're meeting tonight, a house in Montauk."

"How the hell do we get there?"

She looks to Murphy, takes a deep breath, calm and cool.

"If you can get us out of this park alive," Peyton says, pointing toward the roof of the building they came from, "I can get us a ride."

A guy with a baseball bat charges. Murphy lays him out with a single punch.

He hands the bat to Peyton.

"Destroy anything that slows us down."

CHAPTER 37

The elevator dings.

Blood drips.

Peyton pretends to watch the floors light up one by one.

A gloss coats her distant gaze. Murphy can't remember when she last spoke or what she said. He cracks his neck, grips his gun, then fixes his hair.

The fight to escape the park was rough, but Murphy knew what to expect.

Peyton did not, and it shows.

She still clings to the bat, more for comfort than as a weapon.

Dirt mixed with sprays of blood cover their faces. Their clothes hang from their bodies, pulled out of shape by the angry mob. The bones in Murphy's hands ache, ligaments throb and pulse. The punches, the aggression, the push to survive a riot growing in real time, it has taken a toll. He only fired his gun into the air as needed—clearing tactic—a fact Murphy takes some pride in. But the sum of all the violence absorbed and produced weighs heavy.

He wants to use this time to maximize this brief moment of peace.

Deep breaths in and out. He used to work this technique before a job or a drop into a hostile area. He remembers sitting in a helicopter in some third-world shithole waiting to go in. Doesn't remember the job, or the mission, or the reason, but he remembers this exercise of filling up his mental tank. Taking that beat to gather and clear the head. Find calm before the storm.

Closing his eyes, he relaxes his shoulders, breathing in slow and deep.

In and out.

An undisciplined rhythm in search of a steady beat.

"Tell me again." Peyton's voice cracks as she blankly stares at the elevator doors.

"What?"

"When you find her, tell me you'll do the right thing."

Murphy doesn't respond. He doesn't know what he will do. Not sure what the *right thing* even means anymore.

The elevator dings, only a few floors until the roof.

"When we did this. When we combined Murphy and Noah. We did it to create a more balanced, more stable human being. One that had a chance at a peaceful, normal life. And maybe we did. Time will tell."

"Finding murder and mayhem is easier." Checks his Glock. "Stable human being kinda sucks."

"Murphy, please listen." She swallows, turns to him. "The agency? The CIA sponsored company? That's not what they wanted. They wanted killers who could blend in. Mix among the stable human beings and dig in without detection, then slaughter on demand."

"I know what she is."

"You sure about that? Because you have two people in your head does not mean her dual brain is like yours. She was engineered to be deceptive."

Memories of Kate flash. Thoughts of Brubaker pop.

"You should try a little mobility in your consciousness, dear Dr. Peyton." He taps his temple. "So damn entertaining."

Last ding.

They've reached the top floor. The rooftop waits for them beyond the doors. The same roof where Murphy, Peyton, Thompson met earlier. As the doors open, the sounds of a chopper whirl.

Murphy doesn't see Thompson's body. He can only assume this has been dealt with properly.

"Murphy." Peyton presses the down button. "I'm not going with you."

"Why?"

"Doesn't make sense. I can do more here. I'll have a team waiting for you. It'll be small, best they can scramble under the circumstances."

Murphy nods, looking out into the night.

"Promise me."

Murphy doesn't respond.

Peyton stands in front of him, harder to ignore. "If she finishes what she started..."

"Yeah, this all sounds about right."

"If she succeeds? We all lose. Everyone."

"You dick around while I do all the work." He moves past her out of the elevator. "Pretty much sums up our relationship to date."

Peyton slaps her hands on the closing doors, holding them open.

"I'm going to find your kids."

Murphy's heart sinks.

The wind whips around him as the lights from the helicopter strobe the rooftop behind him. The faint sound of sirens wail from the park below. A riot still in session. A drop of blood drips from his fingertips.

The desire to believe her is unbearable.

"Not to be an asshole," Peyton says, "but you

probably should have found out where your kids were before you blew off Thompson's head."

Murphy can't help but crack a smile.

He shrugs. *Oops.*

Peyton shrugs back. *Oops*, indeed.

"Can you find them?" he asks.

"I can. I will. Thompson would keep them close. He loved a good fail-safe."

Murphy nods.

Peyton removes her hands from the elevator doors.

"Don't fuck this up, Murphy," she says.

The doors shut.

CHAPTER 38

The helicopter landed in an abandoned field once used for horse shows.

An open, grassy area a few miles off the water.

Close, but far enough away from the target house.

They came in dark and low on the off chance Brubaker had the heavy tech to track them coming in. Anything and everything is possible considering who she is. She's also traveling with a tech giant with endless resources, and not to mention, they are heading to a house to meet with some of the most influential people in the universe. Brubaker has had more than enough time to work over Eryk Pruitt for everything he has to offer.

Already took Pruitt's hand, if memory serves.

Pruitt's company is the more fuzzy, cuddly company of the Mega Three. Murphy didn't pretend to understand it all, but Eryk's little corporate baby has more of a sales and customer happiness slant to their business. Give them what they want quickly, keep them smiling, and sell everyone everything all the time. Eryk was also, apparently, the only member of the Mega Three who was accessible via a high-end prostitute. Young, ego-fueled, single, and has a stoic history of placing his penis into dicey locations.

The big picture is much clearer to Murphy now.

The helicopter flight was only a little over thirty minutes, but Peyton provided him with some intel on the house and on the other people who will be in the house. He soaked it all in as he traveled across New York, away from Manhattan and into the Hamptons. Past the city's wealth en route to where that same wealth goes to unwind.

Also along for the ride is his Glock, his Ka-Bar and multiple injectors loaded with the same knockout juice as he had in Baghdad. Murphy knows Brubaker had time to gather and move while he and Peyton fought and clawed their way through Central Park.

Murphy used to love this part.

He hums an old Johnny Cash tune as he checks the load on his Glock.

Noah doesn't love any of this, but he's beginning to appreciate his role among the crazy.

Blake Bakshi is the most powerful of the Mega Three.

Not by much, but he has the largest capital size of the companies, with the biggest footprint. While they are all knee deep in tech-generated revenue, his organization writes the songs that make the whole world sing.

They control the internet of things.

The connections and access to that internet, and thus, the heartbeat of the global economy. They were on the ground floor of the mind-blowing G6 networks that reinvented the web a few years ago. A development that wiped out most—if not all—of their competitors. Not a single byte of data can travel on this planet—or any other—without Bakshi's fingerprints all over it.

They also set up several financial firms along the way to help with the mountains of cash they hold. Everything from private equity to questionable auto loans are run through the pipeline. In short, Blake Bakshi holds all the data on every breathing thing.

Eve Ono's company owns the content.

All of it. Every musical note. Every story. Every line of dialogue ever written or spoken on any screen large or tiny is owned by her massive organization. They swallowed up everyone's childhood favorites years ago, and create the favorites for the new and next generations. They took streaming to the next level and are seconds away from piping content directly into human beings' heads.

The last screen available.

The final frontier, if you will. Perhaps most important screen of them all. Tapping into the theater of the mind. Ono is the one who set up the house in Montauk and called this meeting of the Mega Three.

Peyton has declared Thompson an enemy of the state.

She was able to dump his texts and all his emails.

Thompson had direct communication with Eve Ono.

Peyton believes—although she can't prove it given the extreme time crunch—Ono is the link between Peyton's research and the CIA sponsored firm Thompson pushed for. The potential commercial use of Dr. Peyton's work is vast and could spiderweb into many areas, but a deeper understanding of how ideas and thoughts can be transferred from mind to mind perhaps helps Ono most of all. How the mind compiles information inside our heads and plays it back, that's something Ono can mine. That tech is far off, but Peyton's findings are a solid start. A gigantic step. A beginning.

A revolution starts with the first brick thrown.

Ono wants all the bricks.

That plan is also something far removed from the goal of Peyton's research. Far enough removed that it would be difficult to tie it back to Ono—or any of the Mega Three—if things went sideways.

Doesn't get much more sideways than the situation they are in now.

A *we need to meet in a private location and work shit out* type of situation.

Murphy doesn't know everything about global economics. Doesn't give a shit. But he knows enough to imagine the outcome when that globe sees massive blood-soaked riots, then learns that the leaders of the most powerful companies in the universe have been killed in cold blood.

Most companies around the world depend on the Mega Three for their own survival. If the world wakes up to find that the CEOs are dead—more to the point, murdered by an insane domestic terrorist organization—the markets will melt down faster than anyone has ever seen.

Jobs will turn to dust.

It will feel like the earth has been ripped out from under everyone. Financial stability gone. No one will feel safe. The riots will grow until they become the norm. The establishment will eventually lose control. They will not be able to contain them.

A world gutted.

The system cut wide open, with Lady Brubaker holding the knife.

This is her master plan. Her masterpiece.

Now, Murphy has to stop it.

Murphy breathes in deep. He changed into some tactical gear during the flight. Black on black. Lightweight. Works like a second set of skin, designed to move without sound or any drag that might slow him down. A carbon fiber, Kevlar garb that might help keep him alive.

It might not.

He's covered his knife wound with extra padding and injected enough painkiller into his bloodstream to kill all the horses that used to prance around these grounds. Murphy read once how pro and college football players would shoot up back in the day. Large doses of Toradol to numb the injuries so they could play through the pain.

Just enough to get through the game.

Enough to perform, then worry about the damage later. Not the best strategy for long-term health, but Murphy has eyes on the short term tonight. Long term might not be necessary. Murphy is keeping his life choices short and simple.

Get in that house.

Do what needs to be done.

Stay alive.

The *what needs to be done* part is still up for debate.

She will have people of her own in that house. They will try to kill him. She might even try, but he has to talk to her. Needs to know for himself. He needs to be sure about Kate. Owes that to her and their family.

Murphy was told by the chopper pilot there is a tactical team waiting for him.

Peyton said it would be a small team.

Calling it a *small team* is the understatement of the year.

A team of two stands a safe distance from the twirling blades of the helicopter. Murphy recognizes them both from yards away.

He sighs internally. Almost breaks his eyes keeping them from rolling.

One of them is the large man from the hotel room. The one Murphy took out with some smart-ass talk and a whiskey bottle. The other is his dear friend, the heart-eating agent from Baghdad.

Murphy hugs her.

He thumps the large man in the nuts.

"That our ride?" Murphy thumbs toward a white van with a fake plumbing company logo.

They nod.

"Cool." Murphy motions for them to lead the way. "Please, let's enjoy the sweet release of death together."

As they move toward the van, Murphy jams an injector into each of them. His tactical team slumps down to the grass.

Murphy wants to dance this dance alone.

CHAPTER 39

THE HOUSE EVE Ono selected is one of Montauk's iconic Seven Sisters.

A spectacular stretch of moorlands overlooking shadbush-laced dunes with the ocean laid out behind it. They built the seven fabled summer cottages in the late 1880s as an exclusive summer colony for a Montauk land baron and his buddies. The Central Park landscape architect chose the location so each residence could take advantage of the stunning views in every direction.

Murphy picked up these little tidbits while studying the house.

Loves the irony nestled in the details.

A two-point-three-acre property sits on an elevated perch, providing a panoramic view of the Atlantic and a vast expanse of green moors. One hundred acres surrounding the property provide some much-desired privacy.

Perfect, Murphy thinks.

Room to roam, inside and out. Multiple entry points.

Two floors, four bedrooms and just under four thousand square feet of space.

He read that over the last hundred and fortysomething years, these Seven Sisters properties have been home to titans of business, artists, international celebrities, and a long list of legendary douchebags.

And tonight, the celebrated CEOs of the Mega Three might just die here.

Murphy crouches down in the brush just outside the finely kept lawn that surrounds the home. The house is lit up both inside and out, with the curtains drawn closed. He can see shadows of the guests moving inside. Counts the distinct body shapes, and best he can tell there are at least six people inside.

He checks the load again on his Glock, slipping it behind his back.

His Ka-Bar is strapped to his leg, and he added a Defender double-barrel pistol shotgun in case of emergency. He swiped it off the large man after he knocked him out. Murphy wanted to travel light, so the Defender will allow him to go heavy and light at the same time. He loads two shells, one in each barrel, then snaps it shut and slips it into his shoulder holster.

The house is up and in an open area, but private. There are homes close by but still at a safe distance. Yet, with all that known, Murphy wants this to be fast and clean. He wants to be the one dictating the outcome.

Not Brubaker.

He has seen no one come outside, yet. Surprised there is no sign of bodyguards or security for the CEOs. No visual sign of a struggle. Nothing to suggest a fight. The Mega Three are also not expecting anyone. Arrogant enough to think this was an unbreakable secret.

He needs to move fast.

Brubaker will want to do what they came to do and get out quick.

The waves crash in the distance. A cool ocean breeze caresses his face.

Another violent day at a beach house.

Murphy stands up, moving along the perimeter of the land with his Glock held low with both hands. Brubaker wouldn't have time to set up any real security. Possible that they arrived here only minutes before he did. He needs to go in strong. Needs his brain-mate Noah to float toward the back on this one. Noah is fine with that.

Murphy attaches the suppressor to his Glock.

No need to go loud, not tonight, not until he has to.

Murphy picks up speed, running with all he

has toward the back of the house. He plants his back on a few feet of wall between a stained-glass window and the door he knows leads to the kitchen. Controls his breathing. Finds his warrior tunnel vision. Peeking in through the door's small window, he sees the kitchen is empty. He goes to work on the lock.

It clicks

He pulls the door open slow.

Staying low, Glock gripped loose but ready, Murphy moves in, crouching behind the massive kitchen island. There are gleaming silver trays of food everywhere. Fine crystal. Signs of a catered event. The kitchen smells of wine and baking pastries. A whiff of sizzling steak fills his nostrils. Memories enter, then fade.

Something moves in the corner.

Murphy spins, gun raised, tracking.

A woman dressed in a black and white, old-time maid outfit lies tied and gagged in the kitchen's corner. Her frightened eyes beg Murphy for help. He raises his hand, trying to calm her. Offers a soothing expression. Anything to keep her from making more noise. Pointing toward the next room, he asks silently if they are in there.

She nods, eyes bulging.

He mouths a thank you.

He can hear them now. The adrenaline and the mix of his minds must have shut down his hearing briefly. He needs to be better. He can't hear Brubaker yet, but he hears other voices in the dining room. Some speak calm and direct. Others are elevated and panicked. Ones that sound like they are used to being in charge but find themselves in unfamiliar territory.

Part of Murphy wants Brubaker to get away with this.

He can't help it.

If he were being honest, he'd love to watch her plan unfold. Flush it all away. Destroy the system that failed almost everyone. See what flower grows up from a crack in the concrete. They did this to them. They created Brubaker. They built Murphy. Both born from the deaths of Noah and Kate. They should reap the shit out of what they sowed.

A man walks into the kitchen.

A man from the plane and Central Park.

He locks eyes with Murphy. A tiny curl of a smile.

Murphy fires two whispered shots into his sternum, then one between his eyes. He springs up, catching the body before it falls to the tile. Murphy stares into his wide eyes as life drifts away from the man. Murphy's stomach turns. Odd, the sadness he's experiencing. As if he's killed a friend. A friend he's known forever but has never really met.

The woman in the corner cries.

Murphy has no time to console her, or himself.

Time's up. They'll notice this man not returning to the party soon. Murphy lowers the body to the tile. He places a finger to his lips asking for quiet from the maid.

Deep breath.

He moves through the door.

In a blur, Murphy storms into the room. His sight goes white before snapping into focus. The second man from the plane stands two feet in front of him. He goes for his gun. Murphy puts a single bullet in his head. Red mist floats. The man falls back, landing in the middle of the table. Plates launch, then crash. Glasses shatter to the floor. The back of the man's head bleeds out onto the white tablecloth, spreading out like spilled wine into the food and fragments of fine china that litter the table.

Murphy looks over the long dining table, scanning the faces of the Mega Three. All of them stripped of ego and power. Their mouths open, eyes watery and wide. Reduced to their core. No assistants to blame.

No lawyers to call.

Only fear.

At the opposite end of the table a distinguished silver fox of a gentleman rises to his feet. Middle-aged fit. A lawyer at one time perhaps, or some corporate suit before all this happened. Now, he's a crazed mix of what he once was and Murphy.

"Hi." Cheery, gun-raised greeting with a toothy smile.

"Hi." Murphy raises his gun with a cluck of his tongue. "Where is she?"

"Just missed her, friend." Clucks his tongue as Murphy does. "Hungry? There's plenty here."

Bakshi screams something inaudible. The silver fox slaps the taste out of his mouth.

Eve Ono holds her hands together. Fighting to be strong.

"You know you want a piece of them." Silver Fox points out the Mega Three. "I know part of me does."

Murphy wishes he didn't enjoy seeing the Mega Three squirm.

Noah hopes this situation isn't hopeless.

"Again. Where is Brubaker?"

The silver fox shrugs, shifting to his right. Murphy notices something. Something behind the silver fox. Didn't see them at first, but he does now. Bodies lie one on top of the other against the wall. Three men in dark suits, what's left of them. Cut wide open, their insides slipping out onto the floor.

Murphy has his answer on the Mega Three's security.

Pruitt is slumped over at the table to the right of Murphy. His face is pale. His eyes flicker, then close. Murphy presses his fingers to Pruitt's neck.

There's a pulse, faint, barely anything, but he is alive. For the time being.

There's more.

Looking around the table, he now sees the blood on the faces of Bakshi, Ono, and Pruitt. He missed this too. Maybe it was the surge that comes from entering a hostile room. His warrior tunnel vision. Perhaps his mind didn't want him to process these things, but he can't deny what is in front of him. They are all bleeding from their foreheads. Blood slides down into their faces in crimson streaks.

"What?" he lets slip out.

There's a bloody knife resting on the table near the silver fox's hand. He runs his fingers over the bone handle as his warm eyes go cold.

Murphy looks closer at Bakshi. He's shaking uncontrollably. The skin where his hair and forehead meet has been pulled back ever so slightly. On the table in front of Murphy, a bloody knife rests in the hand of the man he shot in the head.

A horrifying idea rockets through Murphy.

"She asked for this?" Murphy resets. "She told you to do this?"

"Group decision, but yes, 'twas her idea." Drops of glee in the silver fox's voice.

The thought chills Murphy to the bone.

It runs Noah over.

She wanted maximum pain and suffering.

"No," he whispers.

Footfalls thump above them. Murphy estimates three more are coming from upstairs.

"This is uncomfortable yet undeniably exhilarating. I know you probably don't feel it, very different for you I'm sure, but this experience is pure electricity for me." The silver fox bounces on the balls of his feet. "Just meeting you is an honor. Man, I wish we could talk for hours—"

Murphy fires three whispered shots into the silver fox.

Grouped tight together in his chest the size of a baby's fist.

"Grab his gun," Murphy tells Ono. She seems the most together at the moment. "Anybody who isn't me walks through that door, kill them."

Murphy pushes through the door returning to the kitchen.

Staying low, he closes his eyes focusing on the sounds above.

Think.

He reviews the layout of the house in his head. There are two ways to get to him. The stairs are in the next room, or if they're feeling spry, they can go out the windows and climb down. He has to assume both are in play. The math on this is simple.

If he's right about there being three of them, two will go one way and one will go the other.

Think.

They are part of him. Part Murphy.

What would I do?

Two will take the stairs. One will—

The kitchen door flings open. Murphy spins. His first shot fires wide, blasting the glass door. Shattered bits bounce and dance at the feet of the maid. His second shot thumps into the wall. A man rushes in. An insane glow to his eyes—could have been an accountant in normal life—his shotgun raised and ready.

The accountant wastes no time going to work.

Shotgun blasts boom like thunder. The island explodes. Plates burst. Silver trays clang to the ceramic tile. Murphy pivots, squeezing off a shot that tears into the accountant's thigh. The accountant drops to one knee but blows out a hole in the wall above Murphy's head. Searing, stray tungsten buckshot cuts into the side of Murphy's face.

Murphy launches out the door into the living room.

His shoulder slams into another man like a runway train. Their bones crunch and crack as they hit the hardwood floor in a pile. The man is enormous. Bald. Looks like he could be a high school coach. Murphy's gun slips from his fingers, bouncing along the floor.

Coach lands a punch to Murphy's jaw.

Murphy returns with a headbutt, then another.

The coach jams his gun to Murphy's face.

Murphy slaps it away at the last second, sending the bullet ripping into the ceiling. Murphy grabs him by the ears, beating his head against the hardwood. Coach levels his weapon.

Murphy snaps coach's neck.

Rapid, pulsing fire comes raining down from the stairs. The relentless fire carves up the couch as Murphy throws his body behind it. Stuffing flutters into the air like snow.

The kitchen door is thrown open.

Murphy twists on his back, pulling his double-barrel pistol shotgun. The blast removes most of the accountant's head.

The automatic fire pounds away from the stairs.

Murphy scrambles on his back using his elbows and heels, pushing himself clear of the couch.

He's created an inch of an angle.

His attacker is at the bottom of the stairs. Murphy can see him now. An ordinary-looking guy, but his face seems half-dead. As if some form of paralysis had set in. He drags one foot behind him. A leg that won't move. Spit flies from his mouth as he screams some form on nonsense, blasting away without focus or aim. Murphy loads fresh shells.

They're not all the same. He's the weakest of the litter.

Brubaker is their alpha.

Murphy aims. *Sorry*, Noah thinks.

He fires.

The thump of the weak one's body on the hardwood floor leaves a dull echo.

Murphy exhales.

Noah processes.

Silence fills the house of Montauk's iconic Seven Sisters.

CHAPTER 40

Murphy took the helicopter back to Manhattan.

The large man and Agent Heart Eater were still out cold in the grass.

He asked the pilot to call someone once they were in the air.

The riot has died down, but one hell of a mess remains. Police and emergency workers scramble in all directions. Chants of triumph. Screams of terror. People run down the streets, racing away from the park. Some run toward it. Others hold phones steady, capturing the insanity of it all.

Murphy cuts through everyone.

Face blank.

Moving toward one place and one place only.

The hotel bar where it all started for him. The windows are shattered. The doors gone. Tables and chairs are overturned, tossed around the place like loose change.

It's dark inside, but the lights from the city's chaos shine through the now open-air bar. Murphy slips behind the bar, grabs a bottle of the good stuff, then heads to the booth he and Dr. Peyton once sat in a lifetime ago.

The booth is shrouded in shadow, but it gives Murphy an agreeable place to sit and think.

Alone.

Unnoticed.

Sirens wail outside the blown-out picture window. Fires burn in the distance. He takes a pull straight from the bottle. Not too much, just a taste. He wants to take his time with this. Unwinding his thoughts—especially thoughts inside his switchblade mind—will be a bit of a chore.

On the helicopter ride back from Montauk, Murphy called in to Peyton about what happened. He did all the talking. Brief sentences. Information cut to the bone, no filler words sprinkled in for comfort. Peyton didn't have a chance to say anything before Murphy ended the call.

Brubaker got away.

The Mega Assholes are alive.

There're some bodies to deal with.

That was it. That was all Murphy felt needed to be said.

Brubaker got away is the part that has dug its way into Murphy's head. A clenching grip on his brain that will not release. There's another thought that grips him while he sits in the dark having a drink in the white leather booth where he was told two people share his skull.

They said he volunteered for this.

Thompson and Peyton both told him that, in some form or fashion. Murphy's mind is clearer now. Access is better, far from perfect, but it is better than it was before. He remembers some things more than others. It's all faint. Beyond fuzzy, but there is a memory of Thompson and Peyton visiting him in prison. Murphy's legs were chained to the floor. His hands locked close together in front of him.

He remembers.

He wanted to kill them both, at first.

They told him about a program they were working on. He told them to *eat shit*.

They told him it was a second chance. Another chance at a life.

Peyton was kind.

Thompson was a prick.

Murphy was silent.

Peyton talked about a chance to right the wrongs of his life. To do better. To be better. She got to Murphy. Even without the benefit of Mr. Nice Guy Noah, her words cut into Murphy's mind. The very idea that he could be better. The thought that he could carve some right among the piles and piles of wrong. It resonated with him.

Prison had allowed him the ability to reset a bit. To let the pills, the booze, let all the rage press pause if only for a moment. Still, Murphy stayed quiet as she spoke. He kept his lips tightly sealed until they brought up his mother.

They said she was locked up, imprisoned because he was careless. Sloppy. *Unhinged*, he called Murphy. Thompson called her an old woman.

Said she would die in prison because of him.

Murphy pulled hard on the irons cuffed to his wrists until they cut deep into his skin. He remembers the look on Peyton's face as she saw the blood drip.

"Sounds fun." That's what Murphy told them that day.

The first day of the rest of his life.

A cool wind brings him back to the bar's white leather booth.

Eyes closed. Shoulders raised, becoming like earrings.

Murphy takes a drink.

"Hi."

Murphy turns so quick whiskey slips out from his lips.

Dr. Peyton stands to the side of the booth with her trusty tablet in hand. She takes one of the few intact glasses from the bar then slides into the booth next to him.

"You can still track me." Murphy pours her a drink.

"I can." Takes a sip. "Did you think I was stupid?"

"She's out there—"

"Yes. And since you didn't feel like talking or answering your phone, that's why I'm here."

"Do you know where she is?"

"Better." She turns to him. "I know where she's going."

Murphy's heart skips a beat. His grip around the bottle tightens.

"She was using Pruitt's unlimited resources to hack into Thompson's data. Took a while, they were working on it ever since Baghdad, but she got what she wanted about thirty seconds before you kicked in the door at Montauk."

"Where?"

"Your girls are in a secure site. Place just over the Queensborough Bridge."

"She's going after them." Shoulders inching up again.

"We were able to track her after the hack. She was rushed, made mistakes. Had everything sent to a phone." Peyton checks her tablet. "She stole a car. We've got eyes on it now. She's headed that way."

"You are a sneaky shit, aren't you?"

"It's impressive the lengths she's gone, but we can't—"

"Choose your words carefully, Dr. Peyton."

"Sorry." She takes a drink. "There are no easy answers here."

"You're going to kill her."

"Not sure we have much of a choice. She's close to the secure site but..." She avoids eye contact. "You can still get there, Murphy."

Peyton points her whiskey glass toward the street.

A black SUV with red and blue lights flashing pulls up to the curb.

"It has a driver with simple orders—ignore laws, get there fast."

"I'm going alone."

"No. I need eyes on you too."

"Where's the trust?"

"Really?"

"How much time do I have?"

"You've got a three-minute head start before I call in a tactical team."

Murphy pushes out from the booth.

Peyton's hands tremble as she drains her drink.

CHAPTER 41

The Queensborough Bridge looms behind Murphy.

As if peeking over his shoulder.

The street is eerily quiet. Cars line the curb, but with no one in sight.

There's an empty city park to his left. A swing creaks, swaying with the breeze.

The events of the evening have sucked the life out of every part of New York and the surrounding areas. Most are staying behind locked doors. Those who wanted or needed to be in tonight's chaos are bloodied, bruised, on the run, in custody, or sadly, dead.

Murphy stays within the shadows.

Keeping himself as tight as he can to the iron fencing that runs along the street. The occasional streetlight slices cones of light every six to eight feet. Plenty of room for Murphy to roam.

The safe house that holds his children is up ahead.

Noah fights every instinct to run full throttle toward the site. Wants to kick in the door. Wants to look into the eyes of his girls. Wants to hold them. Wants everything to be okay. Wants normal to return.

Murphy lets Noah's feelings run, but he's there if he needs to step in.

The balance is tricky.

There are no easy answers here.

Brubaker is here. He knows because Peyton sends him updates on her location. Besides that, he can feel it. Her presence hangs in the thick air. The hair on the back of his neck stands up straight. There's a tingle in his fingertips. He sets the timer on his phone. Countdown begins until the tactical team will arrive.

There are three agents with the girls now, in addition to the nanny that Thompson set up.

If Murphy could kill Thompson again, he would.

Only he'd make it hurt much, much more.

He needs to get to Brubaker before that tactical team comes roaring in. Peyton's only option will be to send in the snipers and assault-gear goons. They will have orders to terminate with extreme prejudice. It occurs to Murphy they might even have the same orders for him. He has to push his paranoia aside, as reasonable as it may be. Has to trust Peyton this time.

Across the street, a warm, inviting light glows in the window.

That's the place.

The secure site that holds his girls.

Their girls.

Murphy takes a deep breath. He steps out into the street, then steps back. Noah almost took over completely, almost ran to the window unchecked. Murphy pulled him back. Impulse control is typically a Murphy-only issue. Nice to see Nice Guy Noah struggles with the limits of the leash sometimes.

He pulls his Glock.

Green means go.

The blinds are closed, but it's like a burning welcome sign for Brubaker. The feds are hoping she will suffer from similar impulse control issues. Hoping this will be too much for her to hold herself back. They are begging her to come in. Lamb to the slaughter. Murphy snickers at the thought. If anyone considers Brubaker a lamb, they need more help than Murphy does.

"Fancy meeting you here."

Brubaker steps out into the light.

She seems happy to see Murphy.

"Hello," he says. "What's new?"

Brubaker smiles a smile so familiar it hurts.

"Missed you at the house party," Murphy says.

"Yeah, had a thing." She thumbs toward the secure site.

Murphy nods, glancing at his phone. Checking the timer as it ticks closer and closer to the tactical team's arrival.

"How long do I have?" she asks.

"Not long."

"Well, okay then."

Brubaker pulls her gun.

He does the same.

The Murphy math is simple. Brubaker's only genuine chance is to kill him and then make a play for the girls. Part of him wants to help her. They can both go through that door, make quick work of the agents. Secure the nanny. Take the girls and go on the run. Maybe Brubaker has some money stashed—she probably does—and maybe they can get out of the country. They can start over. A clean slate.

Why not?

Why can't they make it work?

He thinks of what he saw at the house in Montauk. What happened at Central Park.

Everything.

Still, he has to try.

Murphy lowers his gun. Brubaker keeps her aim dead on him.

"We didn't ask for this. I know." Murphy and Noah talk as one. "They've done horrible, unforgivable things."

"You about done talking your bullshit?"

"I know why you did what you did. You wanted to get us back." Murphy locks on to her eyes. "Me, the girls. All this was to get our family back together again. Each piece you worked carefully. Every step got you a little closer."

"Stop—"

"I get it. Part of me wants to thank you. I want to go back too, but..." He shakes his head, looking toward the light in the window across the street. "This isn't the way."

"*They* did this. Them, not us." Brubaker's chin quivers ever so slightly. "Didn't you see? On the plane, did you see it? The wreck? Did you see all of it?"

Murphy nods.

Kate has to be in there.

There has to be a way to her. Kate can be brought out, he knows it. He can talk to her. Reason with her. This can't be as impossible as it seems. They can help her. It will take time, sure, but Peyton can find a way to make this work.

She can fix it.

"It's not pretty, this life we've been thrown into,

not even close," he says. "But we can find a way. The two of us. Together. We can still figure this out, like we always do."

"Yeah?" She nods, begging to believe. "You really think so?"

"We can get it all back, everything they took from us. But we have to do it the right way."

She's so happy she could burst. She shifts to the right.

A shine of blood gleams as she moves under the streetlights.

Blood's sprayed across her neck and face. On her hands and shirt.

Noah shuts down.

She absorbs the look on his face.

"At that house, I was going to skin the three of them alive." Her lips quiver. "Did you see that too?"

This is what she is now, what she will always be.

"Kate?" escapes his lips.

"Kate's gone." She shrugs as the tears fall. "Sorry."

"So am I."

Murphy's timer goes off.

Brubaker blasts two shots.

The car window behind Murphy explodes as he dives right. Bouncing off the concrete, he flings one injector, then another, with everything he has.

Both stick in Brubaker's throat.

She grabs her neck, coughing, wheezing. She fires another shot that zips up into the night.

Lady Brubaker slumps down into a ball under the streetlights.

Murphy exhales.

CHAPTER 42

Murphy stands alone in front of two graves in Arlington National Cemetery.

One stone reads *Noah J. Alderson.*

The other, *Kate S. Alderson.*

This was Murphy's first request. Well, technically, the second wish he wanted from his personal genie. Dr. Peyton owes him a deep debt. The first wish—to have the explosive removed from his skull —doesn't count. That was granted without a formal request being made. Murphy told Dr. Peyton that Noah's and Kate's bodies were to be buried side by side at the national cemetery where all good soldiers from the nation's conflicts are buried.

Peyton did not argue.

He gave her Brubaker alive to poke and prod.

To study and learn from. To unpack her mind.

He was told the Mega Three were working alongside government leaders to try to calm the world. To tap the brakes on the financial fall. To slow down the spread of the riots. There are talks of stimulus, universal income, zero-interest loans, forgivable loans, and free, advanced training for workers who've been left behind. Changes to the laws and systems that hold people back. A change in thinking of people with money who were shaken to their core.

Wishful thinking, Murphy knows.

All sounds rosy as hell. The devil, as always, is in the details.

The dinner party in Montauk will never be discussed.

Never.

In exchange for her silence, the maid, her family, and future generations of her family will not have to work ever again.

Murphy couldn't care less about any of that. He's served his time.

Punched his clock.

The rest of the world can work out their own shit.

He stares at Kate's grave. A lump in his throat grows to the size of a fist. Noah and Kate's life together rumbles through his wasteland mind. All the time spent, the good and bad shared, the memories all slam together at once. Blending into a rush of colors, sounds and emotion.

A soul-jolting sucker punch landing unblocked.

He thinks of what Lady Brubaker did with the precious pieces of Kate. Of what he saw in that house in Montauk. What she had turned into. He thinks of what he's become, this blend of Noah and Murphy. Hates all that's happened.

Paralyzed by the reality this is really the best he can do. The best play with a bad hand dealt.

He glances toward his own grave—odd doesn't begin to cover it.

The Murphy inside of them can't help feeling the same sense of loss that Noah is experiencing. In a way, Murphy hates Nice Guy Noah for what he's done to him. For introducing him to this kind of thinking. To these kinds of thoughts. These memories. This shit brand of feeling. There's no turning back now. Some things can't be unlearned.

Murphy pulls a bottle of bourbon from a paper bag.

The good stuff.

Cracking open the top, he takes a big swig. He plays back a favorite memory that still rattles inside of him. The one at the bar. The one between Noah and Kate. One that will never be taken from him. His lips move along with the words they said, ones he knows so well.

He pours a long, proper pour onto her grave.

Closing the cap, tears drop down his face. Real ones, not those red ones, thankfully.

His heart shifts to the girls.

"I was right. It's not perfect. Not even close." Murphy closes his eyes, speaking to Kate. "But I did the best I could. Think you'd like them. I checked them out."

That was another thing Murphy told Peyton he needed.

He had to have final approval on the family the girls went to.

He didn't meet them, not formally at least.

Didn't want to.

He poured over the files—five, maybe six times. He dug into the federal background checks, the deep-dive credit checks, detailed audits of their bank statements. Dumped their texts, DMs, and everything else the full power of the mighty United States Central Intelligence Agency could get their prying hands on.

He also watched them—for days.

Stood outside their house night after night.

In the shadows, of course. He's not a lunatic.

He went inside their house while they were away. Looked in the fridge. Checked out the bathroom cabinets for medications that might have been missed. Opened drawers in the nightstands. Checked under beds. Dug around their garage. He followed each of them to their places of work. Watched them drink their coffee. Sat close by as they had lunch. Even watched some of their friends and family for a while.

He did this for three different families.

Until he found the family he deemed acceptable.

The best family—the girls' original one—was not an option.

The fourth family passed his test. People he knew Kate and Noah would like to have as friends, and ones they would've both chosen to look after their children.

If they'd been given a chance to make that choice.

"They're good people. I think they'll take good care of them." Murphy's voice shakes. "I tried to do right by you. Tried to do right by our girls. I think they'll have a shot at the life we wanted for them." Wipes his eyes, resets. "I know we would have given it to them, no question. This way, we know for sure."

He fights back a full-on breakdown.

Murphy helps hold Noah together. *I've got you, man.*

Looking up to the sky—gray with streaks of even darker gray mixed in—the wind blows gently across his face. The cool breeze soothes him. Shutting his eyes again, he takes another hit of bourbon, letting it burn, then looks back to Kate's grave.

"But what really tipped the scales in their favor..." Murphy releases a nervous laugh. "They've got one of those fancy-ass SUVs."

A meaningless wish Noah and Kate talked about all the time. A fancy-ass, driverless SUV that was out of reach for them financially. The weight of the statement is almost too much for Murphy to take.

Yes, too much for Murphy.

The two men have come to an understanding. An agreement. They've gotten to know one another over the last few days. They may not like everything, but this forced roommate situation, this sharing of one head, it's not going away. None of this was requested or wanted—that's for damn sure—but there is nothing they can do about it.

Live together or get damn comfortable with dying.

Simple as that.

Murphy takes one last look at the two graves. He holds his eyes on the four letters that spell out his wife's name.

Kate is gone, Brubaker said.

He holds the moment for a few seconds—too long, perhaps—before turning and walking away. Doesn't know if he'll ever come back here. He'd like to think he will. But life has become unpredictable.

Murphy makes it about three steps, stops, then looks back.

"Oh yeah." Snaps his fingers. "Killed that fucker who put us here. Shot him in the face."

Moving on to another thing he requested from Peyton...

Murphy stands outside the gates of Edna Mahan Correctional Facility for Women in New Jersey.

The bland-bricked prison looms beyond tall metal fencing and barbed wire. Guards move side to side, shifting their weight, watching over things from the towers above. Assault weapons at the ready, their eyes stare out over every inch of the prison yard. Murphy knows this is mostly for show, considering the security AI at these places has the vast majority of the prison's area covered with next-gen scanners, cameras and sensors.

If a cockroach so much as thinks of escape, they will know about it.

Murphy waits, leaning against his new car.

His candy apple red Porsche 911.

Vintage, sweet as hell.

Technically, he supposes this would count as the fourth wish he asked Peyton to grant. But in his mind, this car wraps up into the third. He's going to just keep asking for shit until she says no. Not much reason to make things more complicated than they need to be. This life is damn confusing as it is.

The gates crank and creak as the metal barrier rolls open.

A large female guard holding a single, thin

brown envelope escorts an older woman out through the gates. Older, but not necessarily old.

She gave birth to Murphy when she was young —too young, perhaps—but don't bring that up.

Mother steps out from the gates, then stops in the middle of the street.

Her eyes look over her son.

Almost stabbing at him. More angered disbelief than joy.

Murphy gives her a massive wave with an over-enthusiastic smile. Almost begging to piss her off. She snatches the brown envelope from the thick-handed guard, moving like a cannonball toward Murphy. Stopping only when she stands directly in front of him. He stands a foot taller and has at least a hundred pounds on her, but she could give a shit.

They say nothing.

Neither one giving in.

Murphy would like to think there's a grain or two of gratitude underneath all that tough-as-nails routine. His memories of the woman are coming back to him, slowly but surely.

Some good. Some not so good.

Some flat-out horrible.

But she's all he really has in this world. And he knows he is the same for her.

Murphy cocks his head, motioning for her to get her angry ass into the passenger side. Moving over to the driver's side, he slips down into the black leather. Feels like a glove from heaven. He cranks the engine, letting it roar. Loves it. Rather hear that baby purr than listen to his mother's bullshit.

"You're welcome," Murphy finally says.

"Eat dick," Mother fires back.

Murphy bites his tongue while slipping the Porsche into gear. The prison passes by as he gives the 911 a little gas until Mother's former home is in their rearview. Murphy can see her relax as they slip away, her shoulders inching down as the prison exits from their sight line.

"You're such a sack of shit," she says.

"Now, Mother. I've changed since you last saw me."

"Have to change a lot to upgrade from sack of shit."

"Might shock you, Mother."

"Damn doubtful."

"Got married, had two kids."

She tries to work the math on that. Doesn't add up, and Murphy knows it.

"It's the truth." Clucks his tongue. "Twin girls."

"Wasn't in prison that long, dipshit. Stop your lying."

"Fine. I'm lying."

"*Lying* sack of shit now. Congrats on that."

"Yes, Mother."

"Where we headed in this ass bucket?"

"Don't know, Mother."

"Fucking figures."

She cracks a smile, pats him on the knee, then digs out a single cigarette and thin pack of matches from the brown envelope. A five-dollar bill slides out, emptying the contents of the envelope. She lights her smoke, cracks the window, lets the smoke roll out, then tosses the five-spot at Murphy.

"There. Until we get back on our feet."

"Yes, Mother."

ALSO BY MIKE MCCRARY

Stand Alone Books

Relentless

Genuinely Dangerous

The Steady Teddy Series

Steady Trouble

Steady Madness

Remo Cobb Series

Remo Went Rogue (Book 1)

Remo Went Down (Book 2)

Remo Went Wild (Book 3)

Remo Went Off (Book 4)

ABOUT THE AUTHOR

Mike has been a bartender, dishwasher, investment analyst, and an unpaid Hollywood intern. He's quit corporate America, come back, been fired, promoted, fired, and currently he writes stories about questionable people making questionable decisions. Keep up with Mike at...

www.mikemccrary.com
mccrarynews@mikemccrary.com